SHOWDOWN IN DODGE CITY

The world had turned black and hellish all around me. Right now I could have wept for the Halleys, harsh as they had been to me. But my real grief was for Mr. Ramm, for I figured he must have suffered before he died—suffered so much that he obviously had broken down and told his assailants that Penn Malone had left him a note saying he was gone to Dodge. And then they had knifed him until he was dead.

Whatever had happened, I was obviously being hunted, and hunted seriously, by three brutal men I didn't know, and for reasons of which I had no clue.

And now they were in Dodge....

Other *Leisure* books by Cameron Judd:

CAINE'S TRAIL
THE TREASURE OF JERICHO MOUNTAIN
BAD NIGHT AT DRY CREEK
BEGGAR'S GULCH

MR. LITTLEJOHN

CAMERON JUDD

LEISURE BOOKS NEW YORK CITY

Dedicated with love
to my mother, Louise Judd.

A LEISURE BOOK®

December 2006

Published by

Dorchester Publishing Co., Inc.
200 Madison Avenue
New York, NY 10016

ISBN 0-8439-5282-2

Visit us on the web at www.dorchesterpub.com.

MR. LITTLEJOHN

CHAPTER ONE

Winfred Priddy brought his traveling medicine show to Eldridge the week they buried and resurrected Dixie Trimble. When his big colorful wagon rolled into town, the hole where they had planted her still gaped like an open mouth and folks were rattling on about the awfulness of her premature burial one moment and the marvel of her rescue the next. It was a situation in which a clever man could make good money, for when people are excited they're also gullible, and Priddy was the kind who could smell gullibility from miles away.

I was probably the only soul in Eldridge who hadn't been particularly surprised when Dixie was brought up alive out of her death hole, for Pa had always said the penultimate year of a decade brings unusual things. I had been on the watch for something peculiar since January.

Priddy's wagon rumbled up to Eldridge late in the day while I was in a house that didn't belong to me, looking for something that did. The house was that of Tim and Beulah Pearl and their son, Mark, who was a year older than me and rotten as last Sunday's chicken. Mark had stolen a knife from me earlier in the week—the very knife Pa had left me before they hauled him off to Leavenworth three years ago—and I aimed to get it back. I was running a risk by poking through the Pearls' house, but that knife was important to me. Besides, the Pearls had left their back door open when they had gone off to ogle Dixie, who had replaced last fall's Dull Knife Comanche rampage as the chief talking material of all of Eldridge. I, for one, had no interest in eyeing Dixie any more than I had to, for to me she looked, as the saying goes, like death eating a cracker. But if Dixie was sickly, she at least was lucky on two scores: she had a loud moaning voice and a brave gravedigger. A lot of folks would have run off and kept quiet if they thought they had heard a moan come up from a new grave, but not this digger. He had just spaded Dixie right back up and run onto Rumbough Street shouting the news.

I poked about in Mark's room, in the chest of drawers and the wardrobe. So far no knife, just a half-smoked cigar and a picture under the mattress showing a lady in tights. That figured. Mark always was a nasty-minded fellow, with a mouth as dirty as a privy hole when his folks were out of earshot.

At last I found an old cigar box far back under Mark's bed, and inside it, my knife. I had just folded out the blades to make sure Mark hadn't broken any, which he hadn't, when I heard a rattle at the front door and Tim saying something about Dixie

Trimble surely being guarded by heaven. I dashed quietly down the hall, cut into the kitchen, dropped, and crabbed out toward the back porch through the still-open rear door, which I slid quietly shut just as Tim and his wife came in. I think Tim heard me, for he walked right over, and I barely had time to roll off the porch and down under it before he opened the door and came out, Mark right behind.

"Who's there?" Tim bellowed out in his big operatic voice.

I lay still and tried not to make noise. Tim and Mark walked around up above, the porch floorboards bending a little beneath them. It stunk where I was, for cats had peed down there. I hated to think what else I was lying in.

Beulah joined her menfolk on the porch. "What is it, sweetheart?"

"The breeze shook the door, I think," Tim answered. "I thought it was somebody running out."

Mark said, "Look yonder—medicine wagon coming."

Beulah replied, "So it is. Sure as shooting."

I twisted around a bit under the porch and could see part of the wagon myself—a moving speck of color pulled by two big mules.

"I always like a good medicine show," Beulah said, "as long as they're decent in their entertainment."

"I don't care much for them," Tim returned. "Usually operated by scoundrels. Half or more of the ones we get here have just been run out of Wichita for one thing or another."

"Well, I still like them," Beulah reaffirmed.

She and Tim went back inside. Mark loitered

around a bit longer, walking around right above me. After a minute something brown splattered the ground just off the edge of the porch and a few inches in front of my nose. Mark was chewing twist tobacco. A few minutes later the ugly brown cud thumped to the ground, and Mark went back inside. I waited another five minutes, then shimmied out and ran off. It was dusky dark, and the crickets were beginning to sing. The air smelled like suppertime.

Once I was well away from the Pearl house I relaxed and started walking slowly along, hands in my pockets. The day had been warm, but now was growing cool. All around me stretched Kansas flatlands, golden and majestic in the dimming light. Along the western horizon the sky was an indescribable hue, somewhere between the color of spun gold and that of the hair of a fair-complexioned newborn. I've heard people say that flatland sunsets aren't as worth seeing as those in the mountains, but I've seen both and I know which are best. I always felt that if a man could somehow drink a Kansas sunset, he'd never be thirsty again.

I sauntered onto Rumbough Street, Eldridge's main thoroughfare, and walked along beside the boardwalk. The medicine show wagon had preceded me and was parked across the street in a vacant lot down between Stansdale's Clothing Shop and Rubideck's Restaurant. In front of the wagon a fellow in black pants and a white, balloon-sleeved shirt and arm garters was unhitching the mules, which were already grazing the spring grass at their hooves. The man was stout, with legs like sawed-off telegraph poles. His clothes looked expensive if not neat, and he wore a tall hat that was so battered out of shape and so strangely cocked on his head that it looked like a mushroom growing out of his skull. He was talking as he worked, but all I could make out was a cuss word or two every now and then, which I assumed were directed at the mules. Then I realized there was a second man around the far side of the wagon. Of him I could see nothing but his legs, which were leaner than those of Mr. Mushroom Hat and were rooted down in tall yellow boots.

I leaned against a hitchpost, pulled a splinter from it, and picked my teeth while trying to watch the medicine show men without staring outright. The man on the other side of the wagon came around, and my brows quirked up in surprise. He was well over six feet tall and looked to have inherited his shoulders from an ox that didn't need them anymore. His hair was very long and yellow and hung about his head in the style popularized by the late Hickok. He wore a dirty blue shirt with cut-off sleeves, against which the muscles of his upper arms strained. His chest was broad and thick, his waist narrow. He looked like a strong man I had seen in a circus once—and then my eye fell on the wagon itself and I realized that a strong man was just what he was.

The writing on the wagon said: PRIDDY'S FAMILY ENTERTAINMENT & TONIC SUPPLY, ONLY TRANS-MISSISSIPPI SOURCE OF DR. DEMOREST'S RADICAL PURGE. In smaller letters it continued: A FINE TONIC USED AND SANCTIONED BY THE ROYAL FAMILY OF BRITAIN AND PRES-

IDENT RUTHERFORD B. HAYES. Looking close, I could see even from where I stood that the president's name was a little bigger and darker than the other words, which let me know they had blocked it in over Ulysses S. Grant's name when he went out of office a couple of years back.

A little lower were the words: SEE SHERWOOD FOREST'S MR. J. LITTLEJOHN PERFORM FEETS OF AMAZING STRENGTH. Feets—that's the way they spelled it. WHOLESOME FAMILY ENTERTAINMENT AND HEALTHFUL EXHORTATION. EXTRA ATTRACTION: PHOTOGRAPHS TAKEN FOR MODEST FEE.

Though I was trying not to be obvious about watching the wagon, suddenly Mr. Mushroom Hat turned and eyed me, then motioned me to come. Curious, I headed over.

The wagon, closer up, appeared crude, nothing like fancy show wagons I'd seen before that were like fine mahogany furniture on wheels. This was just a glorified pine box built onto the bed of an old wagon. The paint work was uneven, patchy—not a professional job. The mules pulling the wagon looked fit only to be rations for some starving Indian family, and poor rations at that.

Priddy stuck out his hand. "Winfred Priddy," he said.

The hand was small as a woman's but callused as a blacksmith's. "Pennington Malone," I returned.

Priddy, unlike the resurrected Dixie Trimble, had a descriptively inaccurate surname. Written across his face in pockmarks was the ugly and unerasable signature of childhood smallpox. His nose was bulbous and red, a meaty thing poking out over a dark waxy mustache. His eyes were too small for his head and his head was too small for his shoulders, and all in all he looked like somebody who ought to have bars in front of him. As for Mr. Littlejohn the strong man, he had gone to the back side of the wagon where I couldn't see him.

"Pleased. A question: Coming in, we passed a house with wagons, buggies, horses all around, people crowding in—"

"That would be the Trimble place," I cut in.

"What's the stir?"

I told him about Dixie. His eyes gleamed like cranked-up lantern wicks; he licked his lips beneath his mustache. I could tell he had heard wind of the story already and was just trying to verify it.

"Fascinating!" he said. "Simply fascinating! A true premature burial! You are sure?"

"Yes sir." I knew why he was doubtful. Fear of premature burial was a recurring obsession of the English-speaking world these days. Reports of it came and went, ninety-five percent of them lies. I recalled having recently read in a newspaper about an eighteen-year-old Virginia girl who was thought to have died of neuralgia of the stomach. They had buried her despite one woman screeching that the girl was alive. The night after the burial the family got stirred up by the woman's talk, and they dug up the girl and found she had come awake in the coffin, torn out her hair, ripped up the coffin lining, and scratched her face to pieces before dying for real. Folks blamed the girl's doctor, who had given her a strong dose of morphine shortly before her supposed death—just like Dixie had taken before her own early planting. At that point the newspaper story had begun talking about some entirely vegetable miracle cough cure that contained nothing to put you to sleep and get you buried alive, and I had stopped reading.

I waved at the wagon. "When does the show begin?"

"Tomorrow night, at dark," Priddy said. "A good show, fit for the family." He looked me up and down, eyeing my threadbare clothes. "You have family, Mr. Malone?"

"Call me Penn. My only family is my pa, and he's in the state penitentiary at Leavenworth. He used to write me letters sometimes, but now he quit. He's a common thief. I don't know where my mother is. She ran off with a traveling salesman when I was five years old, and took my sister with her. I live with the local wagonmaker and his wife, but they had a son of their own who died fifteen years ago and they don't find me a fit replacement. I work for the old man. Other than that I'm alone in this old world."

I told him all that because I figured it would soften the heart of the most petrified sinner; I hoped to make Priddy feel sorry for me and give me a coin or two for my woes. But all I got was a cold, flat stare. Maybe Priddy took it all for a lie, which it wasn't, or more likely he just didn't care.

"This Trimble girl—what kind of health is she in now?"

"Terrible. But she's always that way, and sort of seems to enjoy it. She writes poems all about it."

"Poems . . . good ones?"

"Depends on what you like."

"Would she read them from a stage, perhaps? You think she could write one about her experience—a rescue-from-the-bowels-of-the-earth sort of thing?"

I shrugged. "Knowing Dixie and the shape she stays in, she probably knows more about bowel pains than about bowels of the earth. But you could ask her."

"That I shall."

I understood him now: he figured to hire her for his show here. I couldn't fault the idea; a living cadaver such as Dixie would draw plenty of attention.

"Can I meet Mr. Littlejohn?" I asked. The strong man was still at the backside of the wagon, fiddling with something. I wanted to see him closer up.

"Come to the show," Priddy said as he walked away.

I told Old Halley and Mrs. Halley about the medicine show while we ate supper, but they didn't seem interested. They seldom were interested in anything I had to say. But when I told them the show might feature Dixie, they did perk up a bit.

After supper I headed to my room, which was just a shed built at the rear and onto the side of Halley's Wagon Works. The Halleys had a spare room in their house, which stood directly behind the wagon works, but that had been their late son's room and they didn't let me use it. I never had figured out why the old couple had ever agreed to keep me in the first place. As best I could tell, after Pa was put away, the Presbyterian preacher had played on Old Halley's conscience about my pitiable condition until the old man took me out of a combination of guilt and a probable desire for cheap labor in the wagon shop. I told Pa in my letters how they treated me, but it never drew any response from him. The few letters he sent back from the penitentiary never acknowledged my troubles at all. After a while I began to feel like an orphan. Pa's letters came less often and finally stopped. By then it had hardly seemed to matter, for I no longer believed he cared anything about me.

It had come to me a few months ago that I would have no life at all unless I built it myself. I began saving my meager wages from Old Halley and making plans to leave when I had enough to hold me over for a while. I just hoped Old Halley wouldn't get into a rage with me—those were becoming more common now—and wallop me to death with a wagon spoke or something before I had a chance to run off.

Early the next morning, when the smell of dawn still hung in the air like a perfume scent, I finally saw Mr. Littlejohn up close. I was asleep on my bunk when I heard a stirring in the alley outside. I rose, slipped on my shirt and pants, and pulled galluses over my shoulders. I went to the door and cracked it open.

The strong man was out there, washing his face in a bucket sitting atop an upside-down rain barrel. He must have come back into the alley for some privacy. He was no more than fifteen feet away, but was sideways to me and apparently hadn't heard me open the door, for he continued washing without looking up. His galluses hung down past his knees, but his grimy blue shirt was still on.

When he was finished, he ran his wet hands through his long hair and shook his head like a wet-eared dog, then started unbuttoning the shirt.

I must have made a noise, for he wheeled so fast it made me jump. He did two peculiar things then. First, he lunged toward me a little like he was going to grab me. It seemed an instinctive move like a fighter would make. Then he straightened, pulled his shirt back together as fast as he could, as if he was embarrassed, and started buttoning it up.

"Good morning. Didn't mean to disturb you," I said.

Unspeaking, he picked up the bucket, tossed out the water, turned his back on me, and walked off, the bucket swinging and his long hair dripping down on his shoulders.

CHAPTER TWO

I saw the strong man next about an hour after a typically joyless breakfast with the Halleys. I had just left the house when I heard the boom of a drum echoing down the street. I headed for the sound; lots of other curious folks were doing the same.

Mr. Littlejohn was the drummer. He stood on a stage that was folded out from the side of the wagon. It was wide as the wagon itself and rested on big pole supports that fit neatly in slots when it was folded up for travel. With the stage down, the wagon didn't look so crude. There was even a wrinkled red curtain hanging at the back.

Winfred Priddy stood to the side of the stage at a little podium like those you see in country churches. He looked as pompous as a freshly fed bishop.

"Ladies and gentlemen!" he boomed out. "I am Winfred Coleman Priddy, showman of the West, friend of the family, conveyor of health, and for a brief day or two, one of your populace. I join you with my companion, the likes of which, I assure you, you have never seen before!"

At this he gestured at the strong man, who deftly spun his drumsticks between his cigar-sized fingers and did a practiced bow. Though Mr. Littlejohn was smiling, it reminded me of a smile I had once seen a mischievous undertaker put on a corpse: it just wasn't heartfelt. Mr. Littlejohn obviously had become uncomfortable the moment Priddy directed attention to him.

"Have you ever seen such a figure? Not since the days of old has there been a giant so large or a human so powerful!" The description was an exaggeration; Mr. Littlejohn was big, but no giant, though his muscled form was something to see.

"Friends, this modern-day Hercules is a living miracle, made what he is by equal portions of good stock, exercise, healthful eating, and proper medicinal intake. Mr. Littlejohn is an authentic descendant of the famed companion of Sherwood Forest's Robin Hood. He is a muscled marvel, a pinnacle of power, here to demonstrate the astounding potential for strength and vitality built by the creator into the human creature!"

Here the strong man did an impressive drum roll that crescendoed up to a final bang. I had the impression that folks were supposed to applaud at that point in gratitude for the good fortune Priddy was bringing them, but nobody made a sound. Everybody had seen medicine shows before and was waiting for him to get to the part about the tonic he was hawking.

Which he promply did: "And, my friends, we will

present to you a product available nowhere else this side of the Mississippi, one that, when used as prescribed by its inventor, Dr. Cooper Demorest of Baltimore, can provide to you the benefits of a health that age cannot diminish and a vitality that the chilly Kansas wind cannot blast away." Here Priddy dropped his voice so dramatically low it seemed to rumble along the ground. "Dr. Demorest's Radical Purge is a purifying tonic made specifically for the American of the plains. Dr. Demorest is a physician who lost three of his own children to the plagues peculiar to these flat, windswept lands. As he laid the third away to eternal rest, he made a vow. Back to Baltimore I will go and develop a formula to preserve these delicate lives, so easily snuffed away! And this he did . . . and to me alone he has entrusted sales of this potion, this protector and strengthener of life's sweet breath.

"Where does the fountain of life lie, my friends? In the liver! Why else would this organ have the name it does?" He paused to let us think that over; I had to admit it sort of made sense. "Dr. Demorest's formula works through the natural purging of the liver . . . and this without narcotics or morphia. . . ."

The crowd was growing restless now. Somebody yelled: "If Dr. Demorest is so hot for his purge, why ain't he out here selling it himself?"

"A good question, my skeptical friend! The doctor remains in Baltimore, developing Dr. Demorest's Stomach Bitters, a product superior to that of any competitor. When that is done he will join me in bringing that new product to the good people of the West."

"You going to put on a show or not?" another shouted.

"Indeed. Tonight at dark. Free of charge, and of highest quality."

"How much alcohol in that tonic?" somebody else yelled, drawing laughter.

"Only the minimal amount required of any elixir," Priddy promptly shot back. "Dr. Demorest's purpose is the purging, not the pickling, of the liver." That drew another laugh. He probably used that line everywhere he went.

I had been watching the strong man. He was still smiling at the crowd, but still only on the outside. Beneath his pasted-on grin there was something restless and maybe sad, and his eyes, as they darted across the crowd, were fast and nervous as a snake-cornered rabbit's.

I turned around and slipped off toward the wagon shop. Old Halley had decided to keep it closed today, as he did many Fridays since he had started getting up in years, but had told me to straighten it up and sweep it out. As I walked away I heard Priddy saying something about a surprise guest at tonight's show and knew he had gotten to Dixie Trimble sometime last night.

Well, she'd make a crowd-pleasing addition, I figured, though they'd probably have to prop her up on a frame to show her off.

When I finished sweeping, the morning was gone. I went back to my room and dug out some old crackers and cheese from the chest beneath my bunk. Mrs. Halley had been feeling poorly after breakfast and had gone back to bed for a nap, and naps for her lasted two thirds of a day. I wasn't allowed to dig around in her kitchen and thus couldn't make lunch myself—and I sure wouldn't ask Old Halley to fix me something. I kept a little cache of food for just such occasions.

After I ate I went to the well, cranked down a bucket, and brought it up brimming with cold water. I put away three dipperfuls, poured out the bucket, then turned and almost ran square into Ivar Norris, who had crept up silently.

He laughed when I jumped back. I backed up too hard against the mouth of the well, teetered there for a minute, then pulled back up.

"Ivar, I almost fell in!" Ivar merely laughed again. He sneaked as good as an Indian and loved to play this sort of trick on people.

"Calm down, Penn. I'd have caught you," he said. "I came to get you to do me a favor."

"Don't know why I'd do a favor for somebody who'd try to scare me down a well."

"Hush and listen. Somebody said you were a friend of that medicine show barker. Said you were visiting with him right after he came in."

"I talked to him a bit. What's your interest?"

Ivar gave me a surreptitious look. "That Littlejohn fellow—Gene Garfield wants to fight him."

Gene was the biggest man in Eldridge, a raw-boned mountain of gristle and scars who had gone all the way through the worst of the Civil War and had come out still thirsty for blood. He did saddle-work for his living, but made good money on the side by boxing in saloons and back alleys all over

Kansas. It was a popular sport, and Gene was good at it, so good he had nearly killed two opponents in Wichita and been told never to return.

"Why doesn't Gene ask him?" I asked.

"You think anybody would agree to fight if he laid eyes on Gene first? I figure that if you know those folks already, you're the best one to ask."

I thought about it a moment, then said I would do it—for fifty cents.

Ivar's eyes narrowed. "That's robbery, Penn."

I smiled and said, "It runs in my family."

He scowled at me and dug into his pocket.

I could have asked Mr. Littlejohn himself, but I wasn't sure how to approach a man to say there was someone in town who wanted to beat him half to death for money. What if Mr. Littlejohn was the type to take offense at such things? I decided to go to Priddy instead.

But when I got to the show wagon, Priddy was nowhere around. The wagon was closed up tight, though I happened to notice that the back latch was broken so it couldn't be locked. I put my ear to the door and heard deep snores coming from inside. Probably the strong man, considering the volume. I crept quietly away.

Where would I find Priddy? He might be at the Trimble place tutoring Dixie on what to say in the show. If not there, he might be in some restaurant or saloon. My eyes swept the street and came to rest on McKee's Barber Shop, where a man could get clipped, shaved, bathed, and rose watered for two bits. Priddy seemed the rose water type.

I had made a good guess. McKee pointed me to the back, where the three bath stalls stood. McKee was something of an inventor who had rigged a system whereby hot water from a boiler out back fed into a big tank inside. Cold water also fed in to keep the hot water just shy of scalding temperature. Attached to the tank were three big drop arms like those on railroad water tanks. These the bathers in the stalls could pull down to fill the tubs and rinse themselves.

Only one stall curtain was drawn. Cigar smoke rose above it.

"Mr. Priddy?"

"Who's asking?"

"Penn Malone," I said. "I talked to you last night when you pulled in."

A puff or two of smoke rose. I figured he already had misplaced the memory of me and was trying to find it. "Yeah," he muttered a couple of seconds later. "What do you want?"

I leaned close to the curtain. "I'm bringing you a business proposition from some men of the town."

Another puff of smoke, this one bigger. "Come in," he said. "And quick, so you don't let in the cold air."

Priddy was lolled back in a big tin tub like a white fish in a bucket. His knees were bent up and sticking out of the water; his legs were skinny like an old man's. Priddy's hair, wet and parted in the middle by an earlier gush from the water spout above, was plastered to both sides of his head. His cigar was cheap and smelled sulfurous.

"What's this business proposition?"

"A man wants to fight your strong man."

He eyed me without expression. "Young fellow, what kind of businessman do you take me for?"

The question threw me a little. "I don't know, sir."

He dropped his brows and reared up a bit, deliberately haughty. "I'm a peace-loving one," he said. "Brawling with small-town scrappers isn't the kind of proposition that pleases me."

I shrugged. "Sorry I asked, then. I was just trying to help out some folks." I turned to leave.

"Wait, my friend. Wait." I turned again. He thrust his tongue to resettle his cigar, his brows arching in a show of thought.

"Though brawling goes against my grain, my partner does at times take on such assignments—on his own volition, you realize, not mine. I'll mention it to him, see what he says. Actually, I feel sure he will accept." He reached up a sudsy hand, took out his cigar, and waved it toward me. "I'm doing this to save you embarrassment with your friends, you realize."

"You're kind, sir." A tip would have made him seem even kinder, but I couldn't say that.

"You tell your friends to come around behind the wagon during the show tonight while Mr. Littlejohn is doing his act. We'll palaver a little."

"Shouldn't they talk it out with Mr. Littlejohn himself?"

"I'm his manager, boy."

I lingered a little, still hoping for a tip.

"Well?" he asked after a moment, irritably.

I said thank you and walked out, pulling the curtain behind me, but making sure I left a big enough gap to ensure a cool breeze for Priddy. A tip would have saved him that.

* * *

I had been right about Dixie Trimble. She stood on the stage, held up on one side by Mr. Littlejohn and on the other by her mother, and out of her pallid form issued a shaky voice that told of the horrors of the grave, of her thoughts as she lay in the dark ground "surrounded by worm and worry." I figured Priddy had fed her that last line, or maybe she had pulled it from one of her poems.

It struck me as peculiar that Dixie had such clear memories of her living burial, given that she was still very morphined up when they dug her out. Nobody else seemed skeptical, though, if I could judge from the silence of the crowd and the way their faces reflected absolute absorption in every word Dixie squeaked out.

This went on for maybe ten minutes—a surprising length for somebody as puny as Dixie supposedly was. I had always suspected her problems had more to do with the tonics and purges she filled herself with than with true illness, but the one time I had made such a comment at the supper table had resulted in a strong rebuke from Mrs. Halley, so now I kept such thoughts to myself.

When Dixie was done, Priddy and Mr. Littlejohn shuffled her off to sidestage and there made a deliberate show of giving her a big dose of Dr. Cooper Demorest's miracle product. She took it, tilted back her head, and smiled like she was receiving a beatific vision.

Priddy brought the bottle to the front of the stage. "Free of all poisonous elements, my friends, and of all morphia and narcotics. Had Dixie been treated with Dr. Demorest's Radical Purge, she would not have suffered the grim torment she just described."

Here he set down the bottle by his feet and took on a more somber look. "But suffer the torment she did. We may wonder what fate spared her from a horrid and unseen death beneath the earth. Mere good fortune? Trifling luck? So I might have said myself only yesterday, but late last night I unexpectedly discovered the truth." He stopped talking for a full ten seconds, then said, "What I have to show you now may startle some of you, may horrify others . . . but for the God-fearing it will be a source of vindication and inspiration." He paused again, and the people all but hung out their tongues in anticipation of what he was about to say.

"As you see from my sign, I am a traveling photographer as well as a showman and vendor. I took the liberty of making a photograph of Dixie in her home last night and, upon developing it today, saw the reason she was spared. I will share it with you now. I ask you to line up, beginning here . . . that's right, that's right . . . and file one at a time across the stage. Good. That's right . . ."

In the meantime Mr. Littlejohn had moved something out behind Priddy. It was a wooden stand, holding something with a cloth draped over it. I fell in line. Priddy had hooked me like the rest of his fish.

Mrs. Halley had gotten over her ailment in time for the medicine show and by chance or eagerness was the first in line to file onto the stage. Priddy beckoned her forward.

"My dear lady, I will now show you the photograph I took and ask you to tell to the crowd what you see in addition to Dixie herself." He withdrew the cloth. Mrs. Halley leaned forward. The people in the crowd were as silent as pallbearers.

Mrs. Halley looked at the photograph, straightened, and staggered back, her face gone white. Mr. Littlejohn grabbed her to keep her from falling.

"An angel!" she yelled. "An angel right there with her!" She slumped into the strong man's arms. The crowd bellowed out in amazement and surged forward.

CHAPTER THREE

It looked real enough, I'll grant. There was Dixie in the right side of the picture, lying back in her big bed against a headboard the size of an upturned wagon. She looked ghostly herself, but not nearly as much as the thing at the left of the picture: an eerie, transparent woman with wings sticking out of her back.

It was as good a so-called spirit photograph as you'd ever see. I had once read a magazine article about these frauds. Priddy probably had a whole stack of pre-exposed plates stashed back in his wagon, with a supposed angel, ghost, or somesuch on every one. I wanted to ask the people here why they figured Priddy had posed Dixie way off to the side of the picture unless he had known already that he needed to leave room for something else. But of course I didn't. People who raise questions like that are usually unpopular.

Women were fanning themselves, children were crying, and a few were praying aloud in reaction to the photograph. Priddy stood there looking humbled and spiritual, his lips tightly pursed like he was holding in emotion. I glanced at the silent strong man; he was watching the crowd, too, with that same subtle look of sadness I had noted earlier.

"Friends! Friends!" Priddy called, waving his hands. "I beg you, please be calm! There is nothing here to fear, only a clear photographic evidence of that which the faithful have long known—that surrounding us are protective angels, the same angels that watched over Dixie Trimble when she lay beneath the sod."

"I've never seen anything like it!" somebody declared.

"And probably never will again," Priddy returned. "I have long experience in photography, and never before has the spiritual world revealed itself so clearly through my photographic art, though I have seen this phenomenon to some lesser degree. Before this manifestation I stand as humbled and awed as the rest of you. Yet who can say? Perhaps a photograph of your own family would reveal the spirits that guard you, just as this one revealed Dixie's."

I had to give Priddy credit; he had won them over. After Dixie Trimble's resurrection, I suppose, the people of Eldridge were ready to believe about anything you threw at them. I couldn't fully blame them.

I could guess what Priddy would do next: encourage the people to set up appointments to get their own photographs made in hopes that their own protective angels would show themselves, then shift back to pushing his liver tonic and sell bottle after bottle of the stuff.

I circled around behind the wagon to take a chew of tobacco out of the potential view of Mrs. Halley. I meandered around back there, enjoying my chew, and a few minutes later Priddy also came around. He didn't see me, for I had walked back in the dark. He lit a cigar. I could see him fairly clearly in what torchlight spilled around from the wagon front. A moment later Ivar Norris and some others came around. They all shook hands, talked, shook again, and headed back around the front of the wagon. Setting up the fight had not taken long.

I got rid of my tobacco when I heard the crowd exclaiming and clapping, and I cut around to the front to see what was happening.

Mr. Littlejohn was doing strong man tricks. He was lifting a long metal rod that had seats on both ends, with a man in each. He held the bar about neck level and, though he shuddered and strained, did it quite well. He lowered it slowly and the crowd applauded.

He bent some metal bars and broke a few boards, which was fun to watch, but after a while I decided to go back to my room. For some reason, I missed Pa terribly right now. He had always enjoyed a good medicine show. Watching this one just made me think of him, and how he was in the early days, before he got into trouble and heavy drinking, and when he still cared about me.

* * *

In the night I heard something moving down the alley outside. I slipped out of bed and went to the window. Old Halley was sneaking toward the street with his boots off, stepping off wide strides on his tiptoes. I had never known him to tomcat out like that before. Curiosity got to me and I decided to follow.

By the time I was dressed, Old Halley had reached only the end of the alley. He was moving very slowly and carefully; Mrs. Halley, I surmised, had a bigger ring through his nose than I would have guessed. I pulled on my boots and waited until Old Halley turned the corner, then I opened the door and went out.

At the end of the alley I peered around. There he was, heading west in the moonlight at a fast clip. I went out after him, keeping in the darkest places, and well behind.

Something moved to my left. I stopped dead still as a figure appeared on the street. It was Paul Riston, a neighbor. He crept up behind Old Halley, crouched, then jumped forward and said "Boo!" into the old man's ear.

Old Halley yelled, cussed, and wheeled around. Paul burst out laughing, but kept it low.

"Better hush—she'll hear you!" Paul teased.

"I ought to whip you."

"No need for that. We'll see enough whipping tonight as it is. And if your old woman catches you, there'll be another." Paul slapped Old Halley on the back.

I realized we were heading for the fight Priddy had set up. That was an exciting thought, for I had never seen a full-tilt, paid-for betting fight before. I knew from rumor that they often got wild and bloody, for saloon-and-alley fighters weren't much for rules. It usually was gouge and kick and do whatever it took to bring the other fellow down.

Old Halley and Paul walked side by side, talking quietly. At one point Old Halley turned and looked back, maybe having heard me, and I barely managed to dodge behind a bush in time to avoid detection.

We were well out of town now, walking toward the low, rumpled hills northwest of town. An old empty homestead stood out this way, and I guessed that's where the fight was to be.

I saw torchlight when we got close. It made a yellow line along the backside of the crest of the next hill. I heard voices.

Paul and Old Halley went straight along the road and into the little flat-bottomed basin where the empty homestead stood. I cut off the road and went up the hill, moving on around until I could get up on the edge and look over with little chance of being seen from below. Old Halley wouldn't be pleased to catch me here, mostly because he would know I was onto his own sneakiness. But I intended to see this fight.

Tall torches had been planted in the ground around the lot of the stable below, where a rope ring had been thrown up. Priddy stood in one corner with Mr. Littlejohn. In the other was Ivar Norris, and beside him, the grizzlylike, bristle-bearded Gene Garfield. Gene was grinning like a possum. He danced around a little, alternately slapping his right fist into his left palm and wriggling out his fingers to loosen them up. Though he wasn't as tall as

Mr. Littlejohn, he was a good deal wider and mean as a spurring rooster. He was a good fighter who had used his fists since boyhood days when, people said, he had to fend off his father about three times a week just to protect himself. They say that Virge Garfield had been a hard, cruel man, and it was sometimes whispered that the wagon accident that supposedly had killed him might really have been staged by Gene to cover up his murder of Virge. But nobody seemed inclined to pursue the subject.

"Gentlemen, let's get it started!" Ivar yelled, drawing cheers from the all-male crowd. It appeared that half or more of the men of Eldridge were down there.

"We're ready," Priddy returned.

Gene waved a hand the size of my head at his opponent. "Strip that shirt off him," he said. "I want to see what I'm fighting."

Only then did I notice that although Gene was prancing around bare to the waist, the medicine show strong man still wore a shirt. That seemed peculiar, for I had always supposed fighters would want to be unencumbered. Some, I knew, greased their bare skin so their opponents' fists would slide off.

Priddy shook his head. "Mr. Littlejohn insists on fighting with it on."

Gene protested. "No deal. Skin to skin is how I fight."

"The shirt stays, or no fight," Priddy shot back.

Gene and Ivar talked to each other, then Ivar crossed the ring and conferred with Priddy. Mr. Littlejohn watched silently. Ivar frowned but finally nodded, returned to Gene, and whispered to him. Gene nodded too, though he didn't look pleased.

"Shirt can stay," Ivar said. "Let's get rolling."

Ivar turned to the crowd and said, "There are no rules except that all fighting is to be hand-to-hand, and there will be no biting or eye gouging." At that the crowd grumbled unhappily. "Neither fighter shall leave the ring unless he is abdicating to the other. The fight will continue until one or the other cannot rise of his own power. Any knives or other weapons given to either fighter by any other party will result in the fight immediately being called in favor of the uncheating side. Are there any questions?" He waited a second or two. "Good. All betting will now cease." He looked from fighter to fighter. "Gentlemen?" Both gave curt nods. I had the distinct feeling that Gene was looking forward to this much more than Mr. Littlejohn was, though that's not to say Mr. Littlejohn looked afraid, for he obviously wasn't. Not at all.

Ivar raised his right arm. "At the drop of my hand . . . begin!" He slashed down his arm like an axe and danced backward to the rope, then over and out.

Gene leaned forward, spreading his legs and sinking his boulder of a head down between his shoulders. He looked like a fighting dog standing on its back legs.

Mr. Littlejohn wasn't so dramatic. He stood erect but relaxed, moving a little to his right, watching Gene carefully and seriously. It was not like Gene worried him; it was more like he was simply an interesting specimen that merited examination. Gene moved slowly forward and Mr. Littlejohn stopped, waiting. Gene lunged, and Mr. Littlejohn danced to one side so lightly you would have thought he weighed about a hundred pounds instead of the two-fifty-plus he must really have been. Gene swept past him like a bull, and Mr. Littlejohn brought down his right fist between Gene's shoulder blades. Gene's air burst out of his mouth, his voice coming along for the ride. The crowd whooped.

Gene stopped just short of the rope, pivoted, and straightened. Mr. Littlejohn was on the far end of the ring now. Gene got into his crouched stance again and edged forward. Mr. Littlejohn turned that cool, examining gaze on his opponent once more and waited.

Gene got back both his wind and his smile as he advanced. This time he didn't merely lunge like before; he threw himself, aiming for Mr. Littlejohn's knees. The strong man leaped high, at least three feet, bending his knees to his chest. Gene hit the ground on his face, *oof*ed out his breath once more, and then his opponent came down full-weight on the small of his back. Both of Mr. Littlejohn's heels dug into Gene's meaty form. The strong man danced off again, turned, and again waited.

It took Gene several moments to rise, and now he looked really mad. I was glad he didn't have a knife, because if he did I don't doubt he would have killed Mr. Littlejohn right there before us all.

This time Gene did not smile as he advanced, and I got a feeling he had no clear strategy in mind. He just wanted to get his hands on Mr. Littlejohn. The latter seemed to be watching the motions of all Gene's limbs at the same time, ready to respond to a swing or punch from either fist, a kick from either foot, or a poke from either knee.

Gene swung his left fist so fast it was a blur, but Mr. Littlejohn managed to duck the worst of the blow. It glanced off his head, making his blond hair fly but not jarring him much. Gene followed up quickly with his right, but Mr. Littlejohn threw up an arm and deflected the blow. That left Gene off balance. He staggered forward and once more Mr. Littlejohn laid down a mighty blow between Gene's shoulder blades. Then he kicked Gene square in the rump, and Gene fell on his face.

For a moment it was so silent you could hear the crackle of the torches. Gene Garfield was not the kind of man any sane fellow kicked in the pants—the most humiliating kind of kick. Gene would be fury unleashed now. He would kill Mr. Littlejohn with his own hands.

Gene got up, roaring like a burned bear. Mr. Littlejohn gave him that same unconcerned look.

"Let's get this over and done before you get hurt, sweet pea," the strong man said. It was the first time I had heard him talk. His voice was smooth as butter and very mellow; it didn't seem to match the muscled form it issued from.

He had actually mocked Gene! I wondered if he was *trying* to get himself killed.

Gene bellowed and came flailing toward Mr. Littlejohn, who promptly took two solid blows to the gut. I learned the dime novels were wrong—fists against flesh don't make a smack or a slap, but a sound more like feed sacks hitting the dirt floor of a barn.

Despite the blows, Mr. Littlejohn seemed unaffected. He brought up a right-handed haymaker that crunched Gene's chin, then a jab that sank a foot into Gene's hairy belly. By this time, Mr. Littlejohn had his right elbow crooked and poised about level with his own left shoulder, and he swung it around into Gene's temple. Gene shuddered from the blow. When Mr. Littlejohn brought up his knee into Gene's groin, Gene went limp as a beheaded snake. He collapsed to his knees, and Mr. Littlejohn finished him off with a punch that drove his nose back into his face.

It was over. Unexpectedly, rapidly over. Mr. Littlejohn had defeated Gene Garfield and hardly taken a lick himself. And you could tell almost nobody had bet on his victory, for few were the cheers that went up.

But inwardly I sent up a big one. I never had cared much for Gene Garfield, and I admired anyone who could beat him.

CHAPTER FOUR

At the breakfast table the next morning, Old Halley moped like a caged cat. He barely sipped on his coffee and merely picked at his eggs. I figured he had lost money on the fight. Mrs. Halley looked at him, puzzled by his manner. She would never dream her husband would go catting around at night betting on fights—if fight you could properly call last night's one-man massacre at the old homestead.

I sat there wondering if the strong man's name really was Littlejohn, or if that was just something Priddy had thought up so his partner could claim descent from Robin Hood's partner.

"Blast your hide, boy, I told you to pass the butter!"

I almost jumped out of my chair at Old Halley's bellow. He glared across at me out of his deep eye sockets, which this morning were dark-rimmed from his lack of sleep. His lips were pulled back against his teeth the way they always were when he was mad.

"I'm sorry, Mr. Halley," I said, reaching for the butter dish. "I was just daydreaming."

He muttered something about young jackasses with criminal fathers, and Mrs. Halley frowned and clicked her tongue at him. That was the most defense she ever gave me from Old Halley's abuse. But I never held as much of a grudge against her as against him, for I think she was good at heart. She just hadn't been able to throw off the loss of her son, which had built a big wall between her and the world.

Old Halley knifed off a big butter slab and smeared it across his biscuit. The whole thing went in his mouth at once. He chewed on it, stewing in his own ill temper.

I finished my own breakfast. The next moments were strategically crucial. This was Saturday, and Old Halley had not yet assigned me any work. The shop usually was closed Saturdays, but since it had been closed the day before as well, Old Halley might decide we—or at least I—needed to work. But if I could escape the house and get out into town before he thought about it, I had a good chance of enjoying the day free of labor.

I made it out without being called down. Old Halley chewed another biscuit; he seemed to be daydreaming himself now.

I went out to my room, where I pocketed my recovered knife, a little change, and a bag of hard candy.

The morning was bright and clear. I headed down the alley and cut around onto the boardwalk and then down to Ramm's Dry Goods, which had just opened. I loved the look of the building and the smell of cloth and leather in it, but what was in the back was best of all. Nicolas Ramm, the old widower who owned the place, was a man after my own heart, for he loved books. The back of his store served as the town library. He bought all the books himself, those that weren't donated, and handled the loan-outs. I had kept myself from going loco these past three years mostly by losing myself in Mr. Ramm's books.

He was sweeping behind the counter when I entered. "Good morning, Gentleman Penn," he said. He always called me that on first reference, though I never knew why.

"Morning, Mr. Ramm. Did you go to the fight last night?"

"No. Watching two brutes pound each other's flesh isn't my idea of entertainment," he said.

"Garfield's a brute, but not Mr. Littlejohn, I don't think. He beat Garfield without raising a sweat, and made fun of him besides."

Mr. Ramm lifted his brows. Even he was impressed by that. "He must be quite a fellow."

"He is. By the way, I wasn't supposed to be at the fight, and I hid to watch it, so I'd appreciate it if—"

"I have no discussions planned with Mr. Halley," he said. Mr. Ramm was the best friend I had; he knew what my life with Old Halley was like.

"Any new books?" I asked.

"No. But I'm glad you came in. Mark Pearl has been looking for you this morning."

"Oh." The knife felt heavy in my pocket.

"And he had Albert Garfield with him."

My breakfast began to form a knot in my stomach. Albert was Gene's son, a small-scale double of his father in both build and temperament.

"What have you done to stir trouble with those two?" Mr. Ramm asked.

"I haven't done anything to Albert. But Mark stole a knife from me a few days ago, and I stole it back."

"Stole?"

"Sort of. I went into the Pearls' house and got it while they were over gawking at Dixie Trimble."

Mr. Ramm shot me a hard look. "Breaking into a house, even to take something that's yours, could get you in trouble." He paused. "Especially given your father's reputation and the disposition of certain people to look for the same behavior from you."

"I know." I was trying to assess my chances of beating Albert Garfield in a fight. It didn't look good; I wasn't a Mr. Littlejohn.

"You want to stay here until they quit looking?"

"No thanks. But I do appreciate being forewarned."

Outside the street was even brighter than before and there were more people about. I walked over to Priddy's wagon. Other than the two mules grazing on a long rope hitching line, there was no living being around. The padlock on the wagon was closed, even though the damaged latch made it no defense against entry. No snores or sound of movement came from within. Probably Priddy and Littlejohn had checked into the hotel down the street, or were out shooting new spirit pictures at people's houses.

I started around the wagon and saw Albert Garfield walking down the boardwalk on the other side of the street, stumping along like a mobile rain barrel. Mark Pearl walked beside him.

I didn't run from fair fights, but neither did I seek out unfair ones. And I wasn't in the mood for two-to-one odds at the moment. I went back to the wagon door, jiggled the damaged latch, and climbed in the wagon.

It was cool in there, a bit musty, and smelled of sweaty clothing. The interior was more spacious than I had expected, but well packed. Two bedrolls lay rolled up against one wall beneath what looked like a fold-down table on hinges fastened flat up against one sideboard. It probably doubled as a rainy-weather bed for one of the men, too, for there was no room for two bedrolls on the floor.

Most of the rest of the wagon was stacked with boxes, some marked with the Dr. Demorest's label, others filled with canned food and such. A couple of carpetbags sat in one corner, and a small closet at the front of the wagon stood partially ajar and revealed a couple of nice but dirty suits—Priddy's, no doubt—and some big shirts that obviously were Mr. Littlejohn's. A shaving mirror hung on the closet door, between a couple of coal oil lamps clamped into bases built into the sideboard. Toward the rear of the wagon sat a tiny stove hooked to a smoke pipe leading out through the back.

Nothing frilly here, just necessities. The medicine show life obviously wasn't much to brag about for comfort.

I waited, but the longer I did, the madder I got. I didn't like the feeling of hiding from somebody, even somebody as big and mean as Albert Garfield.

If he was going to beat me, let him beat me—I'd do what I could to make him regret it. I opened the back door, looked around, then stepped out.

Mark Pearl came around the other side of the wagon, stopped squarely in front of me, and folded his arms across his chest.

"I want my knife, Penn."

Someone else stepped up behind me. I knew it was Albert from his wheezy breathing.

"The only knife I've got is mine," I said.

"My knife. Albert saw you whittling with it just yesterday."

"I never saw Albert yesterday, and I don't whittle."

Albert came around and leaned his apish face toward mine. "You calling me a liar?"

I was getting more angry. "No. But I am calling you the son of the most humiliated fool in Eldridge—and you're your father's spitting image."

Albert's face clouded up like bad weather. His big arms came out toward my neck, and I ducked. He missed me.

Figuring the unexpected would serve me best, I bypassed Albert and dived at Mark. He hit the ground with a loud grunt. I saw Albert coming at me, and in his hand a blade flashed.

A fistfight I would accept, a knife fight I wouldn't. I had no choice but to run, and I did, hard as I could go toward the street, knowing not even Albert would be fool enough to knife me in front of witnesses.

But I stumbled, which slowed me. And Albert was quick for a brute. He ran around and cut me off, waving the knife toward my throat.

I stopped on my heels and cut left. Albert and

Mark came after me. I dodged into an alley. Mark came around behind me, running as hard as he could.

Before me stood a big stack of lumber, blocking the alley. I had to stop. Mark got to me and yanked me by the back of the collar. I fell, losing a front button off my shirt.

I managed to twist around and land a blow on Mark, but it was poorly aimed and struck him about the chest bone. He laughed and drove his fist into the side of my face. My left ear rang.

Albert came across the pile of lumber. He had run around the other side of the building to block me into the alley. Then he fell on top of me, pushing my head into the dirt. He struck me in the jaw, and I thought I was going to black out.

"I'm going to cut a notch out of his ear!" Albert declared.

"Get my knife from him first," Mark responded. "Then use it on him—that'll teach him!"

"It's not . . . your knife," I slurred out. Albert hit me again.

Mark slapped around on my pockets, feeling for the knife. Albert hit me again and again about the jaws and eyes. I swung up at him, but was in no position to connect. Everything began to grow dim.

Suddenly Albert wasn't on top of me anymore. He had been lifted off as if an eagle had swept down from the sky and snatched him up. At the same time, Mark's hands ceased slapping my pockets. Through the ringing in my ear I heard a muffled yell and lots of ruckus.

I rolled over, gingerly touching my face and

groaning at the pain that brought. The ruckus continued. I looked up.

Mr. Littlejohn had Albert up against the wall. Albert's feet were nearly off the ground; he was straining on his tiptoes. Mark lay face up on the ground, wriggling like a butterfly pinned to a board. Mr. Littlejohn's big foot pressed against his chest and Mark couldn't any more squeeze out of it than he could have wiggled out of a vise.

"What were you two doing to this fine young Christian?" Mr. Littlejohn asked.

"We . . . he . . ." Albert gasped.

"Shut up. Be a good little pile of poop and head home."

"Yes sir. Yes sir," Albert said.

Mr. Littlejohn tossed Albert aside like a dish rag. He let up on Mark's chest; Mark rolled onto his belly and started up. Mr. Littlejohn kicked him in the rump—not as hard as he had kicked Gene Garfield last night, but hard enough to jar him firmly.

I heard myself laugh; it made my battered face hurt even more. Maybe I passed out for a second or two, because the next thing I was aware of was Mr. Littlejohn propping me up against the wall. Through blurry eyes I saw his face looking into mine, checking me for injuries. I heard him say something about getting me home, and I said something about the wagon shop, and then came another gap. When I came around again I was on the floor of the medicine show wagon.

"Drink some of this," Mr. Littlejohn said. He handed me a bottle of Dr. Demorest's Radical Purge.

"My knife . . ." I said.

"What knife?"

I groped at my pocket. It was still there. I smiled crookedly and took a swig from the bottle.

Priddy's claim that Dr. Demorest's Radical Purge contained no narcotics evidently was not true, for it certainly took away all my pain. It also robbed me of what little mental clarity Albert hadn't already beaten out of me. I was vaguely aware of Mr. Little-john putting salve on my bruises, then of walking by his side through town, and of people looking at me with shocked expressions. I smiled back at them, for since drinking the Radical Purge I felt warm and friendly.

Then I was in my bunk back off the wagon shop, with Old Halley looking down on me in obvious disgust. Mrs. Halley was beside him, her hands clasped together and a look of dismay on her face. She was thinking, no doubt, that her departed son would never have gotten into such a mess as this. Mr. Littlejohn was gone.

My ears still rang, but through the ringing I heard the Halleys talking.

"No different from his daddy, and bound for nothing better. Probably get himself hung someday."

"Oh, don't talk so," Mrs. Halley said. "Maybe it wasn't his fault."

"It's his fault, I'll give you assurance. Why do you take up for him so much, anyway?"

"Because he's so pitiful sometimes."

"Pitiful! I'll kick his skinny butt when he wakes up, and then you'll think pitiful! Look—I think he's been drinking—see his eyes? That's it. I'm ridding us of him. They can put him in an orphan home if they want. Or a jail. I've done my part."

"Oh dear, should we be talking so?"

"It's my house and I'll talk like I please."

He stomped off. I was floating in a warm pool, feeling calm and almost blissful. The sting of what I had just heard would not come until later.

For nearly an hour now we had argued and shouted, Old Halley and I. I had said things I should not have. Old Halley told me to put my hands against the wall with my feet back. He held a big board, slapping it into his hand.

Mrs. Halley stood to the side, dabbing at her eyes and making little weeping sounds. Old Halley ordered me against the wall again. I said no, then grabbed the board, wrenched it from him, and flung it across the room. "You'll never hit me again," I said grimly. "Never again."

He shook his finger in my face. "That kind of gall will bring you down, boy! Don't you ever grab nothing out of my hand again!"

"Next time it goes down your throat," I spat back.

"Get back in your bed!" he shouted. "Crawl in and stay there until I tell you to get out!"

"I'll go, but not because you tell me to. I'll go because I'm hurting, and because I want to."

"He's had nothing to eat, dear," Mrs. Halley said softly.

He told her to shut up. She started crying again. I had never cared much for her before, but right now I could have put my arms around her.

I stomped off to my room and climbed into bed. I

didn't bother to undress. My face felt like Indians had danced on it. And now I knew that Halley truly did hate me. Why else would he want to beat me unjustly solely because I had already been beaten unjustly by somebody else?

I fell asleep and dreamed about running away.

CHAPTER FIVE

I stayed in my room the rest of Saturday and all day Sunday, healing and thinking. Mrs. Halley came in a few times, bringing me food, but she had little to say and seemed distracted. I dozed off about six Sunday night and woke up after ten with my stomach empty, my head clear at last, and my mind made up.

I was leaving tonight. I'd not take another attempted beating from Old Halley, nor live another moment under any roof that was his. I would take my meager savings and few possessions and head for Wichita, Ellsworth—no, Dodge City. I had long wanted to see Dodge City.

I crawled out of bed feeling like an old man, stiff in every joint and aching. A glance in the little shaving mirror that hung over my little washbasin showed a face covered with interestingly shaped and colored bruises, like the continents and islands on the painted globe in Mr. Ramm's library.

I dressed slowly, then pulled Pa's old leather bag

from under my bunk and began packing my few clothes. As I packed, the import of what I was doing struck me, and I faltered for a second. Then I thought again about Old Halley and his abuse and knew I couldn't back out. Besides, I was nearly a man now. Pa had taken off on his own when he was just sixteen, younger than me.

Reaching farther under my bunk I drew out a wooden box, reddish and thick with old varnish. I opened it; there lay the gleaming 1875 Remington Pa had given to me just before he was sent off three years ago. Pa was proud of this weapon, which he had bought brand new, and I had always taken good care of it, keeping it oiled up and clean. Old Halley never knew I had it. I had fired the pistol only twice, for I had to slip it out onto the prairie to do it and thus seldom had the chance. I still had two nearly full big boxes of .44–40 Winchester cartridges and a good leather gunbelt for it; that I had kept hidden, too.

I put the pistol and ammunition into my bag, rolled up the gunbelt and put it in, then stuffed a couple of extra shirts on top of it all to hide it. I packed clothing and what little food I had.

It was raining outside, a soft late-spring drizzle. Pulling on my hat, I cracked the door and stepped out. I took a last look back into my old room and swallowed a bit—funny how you can get a bit attached even to a place where you haven't been happy—then crept around and looked at the Halleys' dark house. They always went to bed about nine, so I was sure Old Halley was snoring like a sawmill by now.

I went down the alley and cut to the left. Though I walked with a determined stride I really didn't know what I was going to do. I didn't own a horse and had almost no money. As my mind struggled for a plan, my legs automatically took me to Mr. Ramm's house, which stood on the far end of Rumbough Street. It was small and narrow and turned sideways to the road so that it faced into an alley. When I got there it was dark; Mr. Ramm apparently was in bed.

I hated to bother him, but it didn't seem right to leave without a goodbye, so I knocked. No answer came. "Mr. Ramm?" I softly called out. Still nothing. I tested the door and found it wasn't shut.

It swung open at my touch. "Mr. Ramm?"

I hesitated to enter, but the drizzle was growing cold. Walking in, I saw there was one light burning, sputtering and feeble and apparently in the kitchen. I walked around, hoping Mr. Ramm wasn't jumpy.

"Mr. Ramm, I . . ."

There he was, seated at the table with his chin lolling down on his chest. A kerosene lamp, just about dry and burning out, flickered uncertainly beside him. A mostly empty bottle of gin sat before him and beside an overturned glass. Some kind of book lay there too, with gin spilled over it. I was shocked, for I had never known Mr. Ramm to touch a drop.

I quietly walked over and looked at the book. It was an album filled with old photographs. I remembered then that Mr. Ramm used to take pictures for part of his living, though he had given it up when, he had told me, his camera had been stolen shortly after Mrs. Ramm died.

I looked at the pictures and figured he had lied. The book had at least fifty photographs in it, every one a picture of his late wife. I doubted his camera had been stolen; he had simply lost the only thing he wanted to take pictures of.

I got a napkin and dabbed the spilled gin off the picture album, righted the overturned glass, and put things back like they had been. He never stirred; he was drunk as a heartbroken sailor. It hurt to see him like that. It made me think about how folks can walk around with a sunny disposition, yet have a wagonload of torment hidden down inside that shows itself only in private.

I left him a note: *Gone to Dodge. Tell no one. See you again someday. Penn M.*

I blew out the lamp, mentally said my goodbye to Mr. Ramm, and left. I hoped he wouldn't be embarrassed to find the note and know I had seen him drunk. I hesitated, wondering if I should go back in and retrieve it. But no. I couldn't leave here without letting at least Mr. Ramm know where I was going and that I was all right.

A little crackle of lightning danced across the sky, followed by a peal of thunder. I walked back out to the street and suddenly stopped. Three riders came down the street. They wore slickers and their horses beat a loud, wet rhythm in the mud. Something about them made me wary. I stood very still, hoping that in the darkness they would not notice me, and apparently they didn't.

When they were past I walked farther out on Rumbough Street and looked up and down its dark length. The drizzle was falling off a bit. Off in the empty field sat the medicine show wagon, folded up for the night.

I crossed the street and went to it, thinking of stealing a mule, but hesitant to do it. Near the wagon a makeshift canvas stable for the mules had been thrown up; the mules were inside. The lot was muddy and marked with footprints.

No smoke came from the wagon's stovepipe. No snores or other sounds of occupation filtered out through the sideboard. Priddy and Mr. Littlejohn surely had checked into the hotel, which stood a few buildings down from here. If I were a medicine show man with a few fresh-earned dollars in my pocket, I wouldn't spend any more nights in a cramped wagon than I had to either.

I remembered that the hotel restaurant sometimes set out too-dry biscuits and other such scraps for any vagrant who might want them, and I decided to see if I could gather some extra rations for my trip.

Glad to have found a reason to delay becoming a mule thief, I walked down toward the hotel, approaching from the rear. A light shone in one of the top-floor rooms; the window glowed yellow.

Coming out of the window were voices, muffled, but clearly those of angry men. One voice was Priddy's, the other Mr. Littlejohn's. They were arguing. I heard Priddy cuss, then a smashing noise like somebody had thrown something.

Another light winked on in the building; Calvin

Gross, who ran the hotel, apparently was rising to go quiet the pair.

Sure enough, there was a bowl of day-old biscuits at the back door of the hotel dining hall kitchen, but the drizzle had ruined them. Nothing to do but make do with what little I had and just leave—or maybe be sensible and go back to my room and wait until early morning to leave.

I didn't really like it, but that seemed the best idea. Reluctantly, I headed back toward the wagon shop and had just turned into the alley when I saw a man near the side door that led into my room. He was barely visible in the darkness, but he had on a slicker and I knew he was one of the trio I had seen.

I froze at the end of the alley. The man slowly turned and saw me.

"Hey, boy," he said, almost in a whisper. "Hey, you, come here!" He lifted his hand toward me.

Everything about his dark figure seemed foreboding. It was like encountering a ghost. I backed away, then turned and ran across the street and into the alley where Mr. Littlejohn had saved me from taking a knifing on Saturday. I clambered across the pile of lumber and hid there.

After a moment I lifted my head and looked over. There he was, on the street, looking right and left. The other two joined him. One held a pistol.

Who were they? Why had one been lurking about my room?

I couldn't stay where I was. If they were hunting me, they would find me out here. But now I certainly couldn't go back to my own room.

Only one thing to do. I headed for the medicine show wagon, hoping Priddy hadn't repaired that faulty latch.

The drizzle kicked in harder as I ran. I felt dangerously exposed as I raced across the clearing for the wagon.

The latch hadn't been fixed, thank God. I opened the wagon, shut myself in, and lay down on the floor beneath a big blanket I found crumpled in the corner. I pulled my leather bag close and lay there listening for sounds of human approach. None ever came.

I dreamed I was in the hold of a ship with seamen hoisting sails above and making a lot of noise doing so. I suspected there must be mules in the hold of the vessel, for I heard braying. We began sailing speedily ahead.

A jolt awakened me. It was the wagon, not a ship, that was moving. I sat up in a panic. The wagon made a left turn and rumbled along faster. I wondered how long I had been asleep.

After a couple of minutes of frozen panic I crawled toward the rear and opened the door. The wagon was rolling out of Eldridge; the town quickly receded from me. The mules were going about as fast as mules can go.

A whip cracked and somebody said, "Giddyup! Get on, you wormy flopears!" It was Mr. Littlejohn's voice.

I pulled myself out the door and stood, facing toward the front of the wagon. I held the inside top of the door frame and peered over the top. I saw the strong man's broad shoulders with his long yellow hair fanning down over them. He cracked the whip again and turned to look over his shoulder like maybe he had heard me; I ducked down just in time.

Something was wrong. Where was Priddy? Why was Mr. Littlejohn in such a hurry—and pulling out in the dead of night?

Eldridge disappeared behind me. The road trailed out behind the wagon like ribbon reeled off a spool. I thought about jumping out with my bag, but the prospect of hitting that road at this speed in my bruised condition was not welcome. So I just sat there, looking out the back of the wagon and wondering what the devil was going to happen. I thought again of the three riders. Had they really been looking for me? Or had I imagined it?

The wagon began to slow a mile out of town. This was my chance to get off. I took my bag in hand, poised myself at the door, but then the wagon hit a hole in the road and threw me up against the top of the door frame. I fell out, hit the road with a loud grunt, and rolled at least five feet through mud the texture of fresh cow manure. Somehow I managed to keep hold of my bag.

I lay in the mud a couple of moments, stunned and surprised, but seemingly not hurt by the fall. I tried to rise, but halfway up I slipped and fell face-down in the muck again. When I looked up the wagon had stopped, and Mr. Littlejohn had leaped down from the perch and stood beside it, looking back at me. I couldn't see his expression because of the dark, but I suspected he wasn't happy to see me.

He strode toward me as I scrambled to my feet. He grabbed me by the collar.

"Where did you come from?"

"I was . . . the wagon was open and—"

He pushed me down roughly and swore at me, then turned away, angry and distraught. After a few moments he partially turned again, looking at me over his shoulder.

"You all right?" he asked.

"I'll live," I said. "I'm sorry about being in your wagon. I was trying to get out of the rain to sleep."

"Why weren't you home?"

"It isn't my home anymore."

He waited, wanting more explanation than that. "They don't want me there," I said. "And I'm not a dog to be kicked and beaten because of a sour old man's temper."

Mr. Littlejohn began pacing, his yellow boots making slopping noises on the muddy road, his tension hanging like static in the atmosphere.

The silence became unbearable. I asked, "What's your real name?"

"Jonah Littlejohn," he snapped. Suddenly he spun. "What do you want to know my name for? You got nothing to do with me, no right to be here asking me questions. Get back home where you belong."

I didn't blame him for being mad, but hang it all, I hadn't gone riding off in his wagon on purpose. I was cold, wet, hungry, sore all over, and not sure where I could go or how I would get my next meal. My temper flared.

"I'll go where I please when I please, Mr. Littlejohn. And it won't be back to Eldridge."

"And it won't be in my wagon, either."

"Fine by me. You know what you can do with

your wagon. I'm obliged for you helping me out in Eldridge, and now I'll be obliged to take my leave of you."

I expected to hear him roar back, but the big man grew calmer instead, like he had let out enough steam to ease his boiler pressure. He looked at me, over my head and down the road toward Eldridge, then at me again. His brows worked up and down.

"Where you going, anyway?"

"Dodge."

He nodded as if he almost had expected that answer. "Just my luck," he said. "So am I."

Another time of silence. He kept looking at me like he was struggling with a decision. "You got food for the road?" he asked.

"Not much."

"Money?"

"Not much of that, either."

Once again he didn't say anything for a long time. Finally he said, "Climb aboard, then. There's food and room for two. But if you get in my way I'm booting you off, hear? Well? You want a ride or not?"

"I do," I said. "I'm much obliged."

"Then get aboard," he said, sour as a lemon.

It was dawn before we ate. By then my stomach felt as neglected as a Methodist church in Sodom. Mr. Littlejohn had pulled the wagon far off the road so it was hidden behind a rise in the land that, by Kansas standards, was almost a hill. Then he had given the mules some feed from a sack, unpacked a box of canned foods, and opened a couple of tins of cold beans. He didn't build a fire or ask me to.

I wolfed the beans; a hot steak in Wichita's finest restaurant couldn't have tasted better to me then.

Mr. Littlejohn eyed me as he ate. "That old man of yours beat you after I took you back?"

"He tried. He's not my old man. He just takes care of me."

"You got a father?"

"Yes. He's locked up in Leavenworth. He'll be out in a year or two."

Mr. Littlejohn scraped his spoon around the bottom of his tin, digging for beans stuck there. "No young fellow should have to take a beating from his parents or guardians or whoever. But a lot do, I hear tell."

"Not me. I'm nearly eighteen and I'll consider myself a man from here on out. Old Halley will never put up a hand to hurt me again."

Mr. Littlejohn smiled, which warmed his countenance up considerably. But he still had a stiff, edgy bearing. The more I noticed it, the more something disturbing nagged at the back of my mind. What if he had killed Winfred Priddy up in the hotel? Judging from how they had been arguing, it was conceivable. Maybe that's why we were running like this and staying out of view of the road.

"Well, I hear tell a man can't get to Dodge sitting on his butt," he said. "Let's move on."

"You sure you don't mind me riding with you all that way?"

He shrugged. "It wasn't my plan, but then, I'm not used to traveling alone."

That opened the door to the obvious question: "Where's your partner, anyway?"

His face went cold as a January sky. "We had a few words and a parting of the ways."

"I see." I paused. "He let you take the wagon?"

"He didn't have a choice. I conked him in the head, left him tied up to his bedpost. I don't think he'll wake up for a good while."

I had to smile, picturing Priddy waking up to find himself tied to a bed. But really it wasn't funny, for it meant Priddy would probably get the law after us, or at least come after his wagon himself.

"I suppose you've got a half interest in this wagon, anyway," I ventured hopefully.

He shook his head. "It's all Priddy's," he said. "Or was. Now it's all mine."

Wonderful. I was riding to Dodge in a one hundred percent stolen medicine show wagon that stood out against the prairie landscape like a naked Indian in a row of nuns.

I could back out, I suppose. Take off on my own and leave Mr. Littlejohn to his own affairs.

I could have, but I didn't. Instead I crawled beside him again and we took off again down the trail westward toward Dodge City.

Time and conversation flowed past. I told Mr. Littlejohn about the three riders I had seen. "Do you suppose they were looking for me?" I asked, hoping he would say no.

"Can you figure any reason they would be?"

"Nope."

He shrugged. "It's hard to say, Penn. Maybe they just wanted directions or something."

"With one holding a pistol?"

"Good point." He paused. "Just look at it this

way: If they were looking for you, they didn't find you, and now you're gone."

He was right, and it made me feel better. He snapped the reins and the wagon creaked a little louder as it left Eldridge far behind.

Chapter Six

A full day went by and we encountered no other travelers. The only humans we saw at all were two children who stood in the yard of a little sod house far off the road. The colorful wagon must have been a marvel to them, given the life they led. I'd always found sod houses depressing. Those who lived in them often did too, for relatively often stories would circulate about some father or mother shooting up the family and then killing themselves, sometimes for no apparent reason. I remembered one occasion when a fellow rode into Eldridge with his eyes big with pain and his shoulder split by an axe. He was scared to death and raving about his wife trying to kill him. Sure enough, a couple of hours later she came striding in, axe in hand, looking for him so she could finish the job. It took three men to subdue her, and that at the price of a severed finger for one.

Gradually I became more comfortable with Mr. Littlejohn and asked him about himself. He would answer, yet not completely. And I could tell that despite the fact he had invited me on this journey, he really wasn't happy to have me there.

"What did you and Priddy argue about?" I asked.

Answer: "I have business in Dodge, but he wanted to head toward Kansas City for the rest of the summer."

"Will Priddy send law after us?"

"No. He has cause to steer clear of the law."

"Will he come after us himself?"

"Probably so."

"Where are you from, Mr. Littlejohn?"

"That ain't important."

It was those personal questions he most avoided answering. He learned a lot about me as we talked, even though he didn't seem to care all that much, but I didn't pick up much on him. Which made him all the more interesting, of course.

Toward nightfall my bruises were aching worse, so Mr. Littlejohn sent me into the back of the wagon to rest and take a couple of swigs of Dr. Demorest's for my pains.

The tonic made me warm and content and finally put me to sleep.

I could tell we had left the road from the way the wagon was lurching. Had I been dreaming of my ship ride again I would have thought we had sailed into a storm. I got up, being tossed about considerably, and got the door open. Sure enough, we had turned left off the road and were heading out onto the prairie again, jolting over rocks and clumps of buffalo grass. I looked up over the top of the wagon toward Mr. Littlejohn. Ahead of us was a clump of rocks. It was dusk; the sky was a beautiful violet and glowed like a jewel held to the sun.

Like I had figured he would, Mr. Littlejohn stopped the wagon behind the rocks, hiding us from the road. I climbed down and circled to the front.

"Something wrong?" I asked.

"Just a feeling there might be somebody behind. It's time to stop anyway."

I watched the road for a while, but nobody came along. It grew darker by the minute.

"Can we build a fire?" I asked.

"In the stove we can."

The little stove belched out a nice heat, but it made the wagon too warm and didn't make the outside warm at all, so it was rather wasted. I rolled up my sleeves, sweated, and ate my can of peaches inside the wagon, preferring heat to cold. Mr. Littlejohn stayed outside out of my view. After thirty minutes he still hadn't come back in, so I went out.

It was a clear night, clear enough to see a good stretch in all directions. I circled the wagon and spotted Mr. Littlejohn over in the rocks, crouched down and looking at something.

"Bring a lamp, boy," he called out softly.

I did. He took it from me and waved it out over the ground. I drew in my breath.

It was a corpse, mostly just bone and hide now, slumped back against the rocks. The mouth hung open and empty eye sockets stared at the sky.

Mr. Littlejohn shook his head and pursed his lip. "Froze to death, I'll bet," he said. "Probably wandered off the road in a storm last winter and couldn't find his way back. I hear tell these Kansas winters can freeze a man fast."

"What should we do?" I asked, for it seemed that something as momentous as finding a dead man demanded response.

"Check his pockets for a name, first thing," Mr. Littlejohn said. He pulled back the coat flaps and dug in the inside pockets, where he found a ring and a few coins. With a heave he plopped the body over. There were no pockets left in the trousers, which had rotted away to nothing where his rump had been against the ground. His hipbones poked out through the hole, all the flesh gone from them.

No pack or wallet was there, but something metallic caught both our eyes at the same time.

Mr. Littlejohn reached out and picked it up. A pistol, wrapped up tightly in an oilcloth, with just a part of the butt sticking out and reflecting the lamplight. Mr. Littlejohn unwrapped the pistol. It was a fine 1860 Army Colt, converted from percussion to cartridge fire. It had a brass swivel ring on the butt. The pistol had been well cared for.

"Looks like he put it behind him to keep it protected," Mr. Littlejohn said. "Can you figure that? Man freezing to death and thinking about taking care of his pistol."

"Maybe you go crazy when you freeze," I suggested. "Still, I'd rather freeze than burn, I think."

Mr. Littlejohn said nothing.

We looked at the dead man awhile. "Should we bury him?" I asked at length.

"In the morning. We'll mark his grave by these rocks."

We went back to the wagon, and I was glad to get there. Corpses always did give me the willies.

Sweating and tired, we stood beside the new grave. We had begun digging at dawn and it had taken longer than anticipated, partly because there was only one spade on the wagon, and it was a little one used to dig holes for when outhouses weren't handy.

Mr. Littlejohn did most of the grave digging. He was too impatient to stand by and watch me do it; my way of digging didn't seem to suit him.

When the sod lay back atop the hole and the corpse was covered, I felt better. Sleeping had been difficult the previous night. Knowing the body was propped out there, that mouth gaping open to be a hotel for bugs, put me on edge. And I had half expected all night to see that bone-and-leather head appear and say, "I'd like my pistol back, please."

Mr. Littlejohn took a deep breath. "Well, that's done," he said. He looked back east. "No Winfred Priddys in the horizon this morning," he said. "You ready to go on, Penn?"

"More than ready."

We ate another canned meal—Priddy and Mr. Littlejohn must have lived almost entirely out of cans—and started off. Mr. Littlejohn let me drive the mules this time.

He was smoking a cigar, the first time I had seen him use tobacco. He seemed in a relatively good humor now, like he was warming to me.

"You know, if Winfred were here, he'd have taken pictures of that body to use for a ghost on his spirit plates," Mr. Littlejohn said. He was half smiling, talking about Priddy almost fondly, which struck me as odd, given that he had tied up the man and stolen his wagon.

"Yeah," I said. "What's he do—double expose?"

"I don't know what you call it."

We rode and Mr. Littlejohn smoked. The more I was around him, the more interesting and yet mysterious he seemed. I decided to dig for more information. "How'd you get to be a strong man?" I asked.

"I had some opportunities for lots of exercise."

Typical vague Jonah Littlejohn answer.

"How'd you meet Priddy?"

"I ran across him one day."

"You got work waiting in Dodge?"

"Nope. Just somebody I need to look up."

I shifted on my seat. "You sure don't have a lot to tell about yourself."

"Nothing worth the telling."

Mr. Littlejohn's good spirits faded dramatically the closer we got to Dodge. By dusk, when we camped again, he was very withdrawn and somber. I wondered if my prodding about his past had set him to thinking over unpleasant memories. Something obviously was weighing on his mind.

It made me apprehensive to see him like he was. When he crawled into the wagon and came out with a bottle of whiskey, a dark dread came over me. It reminded me of Pa as he had been right before he went outlaw—drinking, trying to baptize himself in liquor for whatever failings he had.

I watched Mr. Littlejohn drink for the next hour and hoped he wasn't a mean drunk, strong as he was. As he drank, he cleaned the pistol we had found, I was glad he had no ammunition to fit it. At first it seemed the liquor was just drawing him deeper into himself, but all at once he seemed to become aware of me, turned on me, and said, "What are you so goggle-eyed at, boy?"

I looked away.

"I asked you a question!"

"Just watching you. Sorry." He seemed like a different man than before.

"Watching me!" He snorted sarcastically, then caricatured my voice: "Just watching you. Sorry."

Now it starts, I thought. Just like Pa.

"Don't you figure a man who works up on a stage gets a little tired of being watched all the time? Don't you figure he gets weary of folks ogling him like a calf at an auction?"

I said nothing.

"You deaf, boy?"

"Yes, I suppose he does," I said.

He mocked my voice again: "Yes, I suppose he does."

He stood up, wavered like a big oak in a storm, then began walking about, waving his bottle. "I never really wanted to be a showman, you know. Getting up in front of a gaggle of gaping fools never thrilled my soul, I'll tell you. I'm through with it. Through with Winfred Priddy and living out of a can and putting up with bug-eyed runts who watch a man when he don't want to be watched. You hear me, boy? You understand that?"

"Yes sir."

He gave me a long, searching stare. "I ought to throw you out," he said. "Throw your butt out on this prairie and make you walk to Dodge. You got no right to be here."

"No sir, I reckon I don't," I said. I felt a twinge of rising anger.

He mocked my voice again.

"You got no cause to do that," I said.

It went all over him. He gave me the most hateful, frightening look I'd ever seen and pointed a long finger at my face.

"You get your little leather bag and get out of my sight! Now!"

I admit that surprised me. I didn't think he'd *really* throw me off in the middle of night and nowhere. But I sure wasn't about to beg a raging drunk for mercy.

"All right," I said, standing. "I'll go right now."

"You do that."

I opened the wagon and fished out my bag. I was mad now and would have walked away even if this were the dead of winter and a blizzard were howling. Mr. Littlejohn's rampage had brought back all my worst memories of Pa's drinking days. I wouldn't stay around for any drunkard to abuse, any more than I would have stayed in Eldridge for Old Halley to beat on.

"Maybe I'll see you in Dodge," I said.

He took a big swig from his bottle and coughed. "Get out of my sight," he ordered once more.

I stomped off through the buffalo grass; a ways

out I looked back. In the moonlight I could just make out Mr. Littlejohn and the wagon. He was standing, looking after me. It was a sad, lonely scene—his tall figure, the dark wagon, the open flatland stretching all around beneath the wide sky.

"Wait!" he hollered after me. "Don't go."

I didn't respond.

"Ain't no need for this, boy!"

Still I continued.

He didn't say anything more until I was a long way off. I could barely hear his voice: "Get on, then, you young jackass! Rot out there if you want!"

I kept walking.

Leaving wasn't the smartest thing I had ever done, but then, people seldom do smart things when they're mad.

I had only one thin blanket in my bag, and it wasn't much against the cool night. I made my bed in a low place near the road, shivering and never really sleeping.

When morning came, I continued walking. My stomach was empty and I felt light-headed. I found a few crackers in my pouch and ate them.

An hour later I heard the sound of the medicine show wagon coming up behind. The trail had just come over a little rise, so I was hidden from Mr. Littlejohn's view when the first noise reached me. I darted off the trail and dropped into an old buffalo wallow, peering up over the edge.

The wagon came over the rise. Mr. Littlejohn looked the worse for his night of drinking. He must have seen my tracks or sensed I was near, for he stopped the wagon, stood on the seat, and scanned the prairie all around. I lay low, wondering if I wouldn't be better off to let him see me. But I wouldn't. A man who drinks one night will drink another, and if he'll hit you with words once, the next time he'll do it with fists. Besides, I was still plain mad at him.

"Boy?" Mr. Littlejohn called. "Boy?"

At last he sat again and started off. I let him get far ahead, then rose and got on the trail again.

I wondered how close I was, and how well I would make it with almost nothing to eat. I should have taken some cans of food when I left Mr. Littlejohn, but I had been too worked up to think of it at the time. Besides, he probably wouldn't have let me.

The morning grew hotter, my bag heavier. I shifted it from hand to hand. The sun burned down on me. It didn't seem so much like spring as summer today. I kept my mind on Dodge, mostly to keep it off my vacant belly. I would be reaching the town just before the first cattle from Texas lumbered in. It would be a wild time in the cowtown. Everybody knew the reputation of Dodge; folks in Eldridge and other Kansas towns often downtalked Dodge for catering to the baser side of humanity, all for the sake of the Texas cowboy's dollar. It would be interesting to see how much of the talk was true—if I could make it there before I dropped from hunger.

Or thirst. I didn't even have a canteen. The more I thought about it, the more I wished I had let Mr. Littlejohn find me. Maybe if I walked as hard and quickly as I could I would run into him later when he camped for the night. Packing away my pride and anger, I decided to try.

I grew more tired and hungry. Mr. Littlejohn's wagon tracks stretched ahead of me and made me wonder how long it would take to catch up with him.

The day wore on, every hour twice as long as usual. Near sunset I had forgotten my hunger, but thirst was unbearable. As the day grew duskier I at last saw where Mr. Littlejohn's wagon tracks had again left the road. Looking across the plains, I could not see the wagon, though; he must have parked it behind a rock or rise, like before. I had one final doubt about the wisdom of rejoining him, but the demon spreading thirsty sand across my throat overruled the doubt. I started walking through the buffalo grass.

I hadn't gotten more than ten yards before I heard a sound from the trail behind me. A wagon, but one that rumbled, squeaked, creaked, clattered . . . and rattled peculiarly. Down the road I could just make it out now—a spot growing gradually bigger in the declining light.

This was the time just before darkness comes when the land and sky change, making surroundings that one moment before seemed as familiar as an old hat seem the next moment to be transformed and unknown—like nature has suddenly put on a scary mask, or maybe taken off a friendly-looking one to show you the true, cruel face beneath. This was what Pa had always called the dead hour, the time of day old people are most apt to die, and babies to come out stillborn.

Maybe that's what made the thing I saw coming toward me seem so awesome and morbid.

It was a very long wagon pulled by three teams of mules. Driving it was a human piece of gristle, iron, and muscle with a bearded head stuck on top. He cracked his whip and hollered for the mules to tuck up there, his voice booming like a bass drum.

The wagon was heaped with bones. Hundreds of them. They accounted for the peculiar rattling I had heard. The sight put cold fingers on the back of my neck. I thought of the old tale of Hades riding out of the earth in his chariot to capture Persephone.

I stood by the road as the wagon drew near. The man apparently noticed me only then, for he looked startled. Then a big grin spread across his face. He pulled the wagon to a stop. Some of the bones popped and rattled and resettled themselves.

"Howdy, son," he said. "Mite late to be walking alone."

"It is at that," I said.

"You thirsty?"

"I am."

"Come up here and have yourself some water with old Primo Smith." He pronounced the name *pry-mo*. "I been wishing for some company. Going to Dodge?"

It was almost dark, and Primo Smith's grin seemed brighter than the rim of sun that was just now smoldering out on the western skyline. I grinned too, and noticed that nature had suddenly put on its friendly face again. Even the heap of buffalo bones didn't look ominous anymore.

"I'm obliged," I said. "I am walking to Dodge."

"You're riding now, with old Primo," he said. "What's your name?"

"Penn . . ." I started to say Malone, but suddenly realized there was no reason to reveal too much about myself. Too late on my first name, but at least I could change the last one. ". . . Corey. Penn Corey." Corey had been my mother's maiden name; it was the only name I could pull from the air at the moment.

"It's a pleasure, Penn."

I settled onto the seat. The water was so good I didn't even mind the brown dried tobacco crust around the canteen mouth. I took a long, cool swallow.

"Jerked longhorn beef in the bag at your feet," Primo said. "It ain't no cafe meal, but it will fill a gut."

He leaned to the left, spit out a long stream of tobacco, and whipped up the mules again.

CHAPTER SEVEN

I had never met a friendlier man than Primo Smith. He smiled and whistled endlessly, and treated me like a friend from the outset. We rode for maybe an hour before stopping—I never spotted Mr. Little-john's wagon, though I looked for it. The next day we pushed hard, hoping to reach Dodge by dark.

I told Primo a bit about myself, but only a bit— that I was bound for Dodge, that I hoped to find work, that I was on my own, and that my previous transportation hadn't worked out. I explained my now-fading bruises as the result of an accident, but had the impression he didn't buy that, though he made no comment.

Mostly I didn't talk, but listened, for Primo was full of words and stories that apparently had gotten all bottled up while he was bone hunting alone these past days. Once he let them loose they poured out like chickens from a burning coop.

He told about himself and his former buffalo

hunting friends in Dodge's older days, when buffalo herds in the area had stretched for miles, and a man could make in a day of hunting what it took a cowboy weeks of hard cattle driving to earn today.

Among Primo's old hunting companions, I learned, had been Bat Masterson and his brother, Ed, who later made names for themselves as peace officers in and around Dodge. Bat had for more than a year now been sheriff of Ford County, of which Dodge was the seat, and just recently had been named a deputy U.S. marshal as well, replacing a previous one, who had been named McCarty. As sometimes happened to men of the law on the frontier, McCarty had been gunned down by an unruly drunk, this one a cow camp cook.

A similar fate had befallen Ed Masterson, Bat's older brother, in April a year ago. Primo mentioned it, and I remembered reading about it in the papers. Ed had been the newly elected town marshal in Dodge when a drunk cowboy had shot him through the abdomen at a range so close it had set his clothes on fire. He had died after a few minutes, and they had buried him with honor at nearby Fort Dodge.

Primo obviously had thought highly of Ed and had even greater appreciation for Bat, who he said had saved his scalp when the two fought Indians together at Adobe Walls.

"Dodge must be as wild as they say, then," I commented after Primo told about the murdered peace officers.

"It's wild at times, but no more than your typical cattle town, I don't think," Primo said. "Them cowboys come in after long stretches on the trail, ready to stretch theirselves a bit, and Dodge welcomes them to do it. Dang, the whole town is built around the Texas cattle business. But to tell you the truth, Dodge was wilder back in the buffalo hunting days. There was no law at all then for two, three years, nothing but man-to-man kind of law, that is, and that's the sternest kind . . . but I miss them days, I do. I'd turn back the clock if I could."

"What do you do with all these bones?" I asked.

"Sell 'em. There's dealers right there at the railroad tracks. They send them back east to make sugar and fertilizer and pretty combs for the ladies. What's piled on this wagon is just about all that's left of the buffalo days, son, and soon even the bones will be gone. That's a sad thing for old Primo to think about." He grinned. "So I don't."

As time passed, I would find that attitude pretty well summed up Primo Smith. What was unpleasant simply wasn't worth thinking about, in his book.

"You still think we'll get to Dodge today?" I asked through a yawn. It was not yet noon, but we had slept only a few hours the previous night. Primo had bounded out of his blankets well before the sun was up, eager to hitch up and roll at first light.

"We're right on schedule," he said. "If we're lucky we can get these bones unloaded and I'll have some cash in my pocket, and I'll pay you for your unloading help."

"Obliged," I said. "But I owe you that for free in return for the ride."

"No man works for Primo what doesn't get cash pay," he said.

I didn't argue, for I did need money. The few dollars I had managed to save felt terribly meager in my pocket. They wouldn't keep me fed and housed for long. I wondered if work would be hard to come by in Dodge.

Primo started talking about the old days again. He had first come to Dodge in '72, the year a group of businessmen and some officers from Fort Dodge decided a town was needed, partly to provide a recreational place for the soldiers, but also because the area was a likely spot for development once the railroad came in. They picked a site upriver from the fort and declared it a city—Buffalo City, they started to call it before deciding on the name Dodge City.

The town stood in the buffalo country on the north bank of the Arkansas River. Buffalo herds in those days were so big, Primo said, that the sound they made was like thunder echoing on top of itself hundreds, thousands of times. Primo called it a frightening but sweet sound, one he'd give up an arm to hear again.

When the Santa Fe railroad came in, Dodge became an important railhead, as its developers had hoped. Primo and his fellow hunters slaughtered buffalo by the millions; the government encouraged such not only as good prairie business, but as a way of opening up the plains for settlement.

"That first winter, I remember, there were mountains of hides by the Santa Fe tracks," Primo said. "Thousands upon thousands of them, heaped up to go east. You'll never see the like of it again, Penn. Now there's no hides, just bones like these we're hauling."

As the buffalo had declined, the cattle industry

had grown. Cattlemen from Texas began driving longhorns up the Great Western Trail from Texas. Upon reaching Dodge, cattlemen could load the herds onto the Santa Fe to go back east, or continue on to Ogallala in Nebraska, if they preferred the Union Pacific line. Another alternative at Ogallala was to head up one fork of the trail to Fort Buford in Dakota, or on the other to Wyoming or Montana.

The day wore on. We rested the mules and ate in the afternoon. I was getting fidgety, excited about Dodge. But it was also becoming clear to me how big a decision I had made when I left the Halleys, and how serious a hand fate had dealt me when I hitched a ride first with Jonah Littlejohn, then with Primo. I was a little worried. I might get to Dodge and starve. Maybe another gang of Indians would come through and kill and scalp like the Dull Knife band had done here just last year. Maybe some drunk cowboy would shoot at another marshal and hit me instead. I could without strain think of a hundred sad fates for myself. But there was no turning back now. And the truth was, despite my fears a sense of adventure was beginning to grow.

I was almost to the town Kansans talked about more than any other, I had at least a few dollars and the promise of a few more—and I wasn't even downtrodden young Penn Malone the boy anymore, but Penn Corey the free man, drifter, and adventurer. And I had already found at least one friend in Primo. And perhaps a second in Mr. Littlejohn, at least in his sober version. Only time would tell.

I looked about, trying again to spot the medicine show wagon, but did not.

In any case, it was likely I would see Mr. Littlejohn again after we reached Dodge. The town wasn't all that big, and Jonah Littlejohn would have stood out in a big city.

We passed Fort Dodge and approached Dodge City along the Santa Fe tracks. East of town we passed little groups of dugout houses with dirt roofs and trash strewn about. Every now and then somebody would appear and wave or holler in a friendly way at Primo.

"How far?" I asked, squinting into the westering sun.

"About a mile," Primo said. "Dang, I'm thirsty. Can't wait to hit them saloons."

It was almost dark when I caught first sight of Dodge City, and at this hour I couldn't tell much about it. It looked to be mostly dark buildings with yellow lighted windows, and from what I could tell was basically like scores of other western towns. There were stock pens north of the tracks, and around the telegraph poles stood a mountain of bones like those we were hauling. Primo rolled up close to the pile and hopped down; a man emerged from a building and they talked. I climbed down and waited.

"Let's get her done, Penn," Primo called.

As I tossed out bones I was amazed at the way life progresses. Last week at this time I was curled up in my bunk, counting my money and wondering if I would ever truly pull free from the Halleys. Now, here I was, tossing off old buffalo bones at the railhead of the wickedest city on the western Kansas plains.

When we were finished I was winded and sat against the sideboard of the wagon while Primo dealt with the bone buyer. He came back with a full pocket and a broad grin and beckoned me up onto the seat.

"That makes right at twenty five ton I've hauled in. Eight dollars a ton, and that gives me two hundred dollars. Dang, Penn, that's good wages compared to what them cowboys who ride in here all summer get. And in a couple of days I'll go out and get more bones, make some more money. I figure that's grounds for celebration. What do you say?"

Right then I saw that by leaving Mr. Littlejohn I had not freed myself of the company of drunks; I would soon have another on my hands. But I had nowhere else to go and nothing else to do. "Whatever you want, Primo."

First we went to Primo's home. Primo lived on Third Avenue, which we reached by riding along Front Street and turning right. I got a good view of Dodge and its nocturnal population. We passed the Dodge House Hotel, Mueller's Boot Shop, the Lone Star and Long Branch saloons, numerous other businesses. The Long Branch had a new coat of paint you could smell from the street. As before, people all along the way waved and shouted greetings to Primo. He obviously was well liked.

"How many saloons you got here?" I asked him.

He wrinkled up his brow, counting. "Fourteen, fifteen, something like that. Newest is the Hub. This town's greasing its gears for the cattle season, Penn. Big money around here come summer."

We turned up Third Avenue, crossed two more

streets, and came to Primo's residence about half a block up. It was a dugout similar to those we had passed east of town and was turned backward to the street.

The interior of the dugout stunk. The corners were full of rat droppings, and one wall was papered with rattlesnake skins, pegged up like decorations. Clothing lay about, intermingled with dirty dishes and general garbage. Primo lit a lamp and literally kicked his way in through the mess like a buffalo plowing through a snowbank. He left a pathway behind him.

"Make yourself at home," he said, then went back out to unhitch his mules. I followed him out, seeing nothing inside to make me want to stay. He turned the mules into a stock pen built behind his home and fed them out of a small stable on the far end.

"Time for some fun," he said, then paused. "Dang, Penn, I almost forgot." He pulled five dollars from his pocket and handed it to me. "There's your pay."

I shook my head. "That's way too much, Primo."

"Take it. In a few days I'll head out, get more bones, make more money. Anyway, I appreciated your company on the road as much as your work. If it bothers you, buy me a drink."

We walked back toward Front Street, passing houses and businesses along the way. We approached the Long Branch.

"This where we're going?"

"Nah. Too uppity for me. I'm more comfortable south of the dead line."

"What's the dead line?"

"The line beyond which a man can fully relax," he said, and explained no further.

What the dead line was, I learned, was the Santa Fe tracks, south of which the town ordinance against carrying firearms was usually ignored and carousing went on full steam. We made the rounds and wound up in the Lady Gay Dance Hall, which was crowded and hot tonight. A woman was singing on the stage, couples were dancing, several in various stages of inebriation, and a line of drinkers stood at the bar. Primo was amazed and almost offended when I declined to drink anything other than coffee. I held liquor responsible for most of Pa's troubles and seldom touched it myself.

Primo had just finished explaining the dead line to me. "Like I said, a man can really relax south of the line," he commented in conclusion.

I looked around. "Sounds to me like a man can get killed easier south of the line, too."

"That's sometimes a fact," Primo said. "But north of the line has its fair share of such, too. That's where McCarty, the marshal, got killed. And Levi Richardson, just a few days back. He was a friend of mine, Levi."

Half an hour later Primo was well on his way to a good, solid drunk. I had another cup of coffee and thought about going home, then realized I had no home to go to—unless Primo invited me to stay at his place, which so far he hadn't done except in an implied way. I didn't want to ask about it right out for fear of seeming pushy.

A drunk came along and bought Primo a new

round. The two meandered through a slurred and rather nonsensical exchange, then the drunk wandered off to dance with a painted-up fat woman. Another man came up and also bought Primo a drink, then left. It happened a third time. Primo was having the evening of his life while spending hardly a cent.

I saw that Primo was something of a pet in Dodge, a jolly sort of coot people liked to joke and drink with. But I could detect an edge of patronization in the way some talked to him. People do that around those they consider of inferior intelligence; hearing such directed at Primo confirmed a conclusion: Primo was likable but not particularly smart.

Another man came toward us. He was smiling; his bleary, red eyes indicated that he, like most everybody else, was deeply into his cups. He clapped a hand down on Primo's shoulder. Primo turned and smiled.

"Moon Price, I ain't seen you in a month of Sundays!"

"How are you, Primo?"

"Been out bone collecting. I'm rich now. This here's my friend . . ." He hesitated, trying to think of my name.

"Penn Corey," I said.

"Penn Corey," Primo repeated. The other man nodded, then promptly ignored me.

"You say you're rich?"

"Sure am," Primo said.

"Then you can pay me that thirty dollars you owe me."

"What thirty dollars?"

"That I lent you six months back."

Primo frowned, digging back into his mind. "I done paid that back, Moon. Paid it back long ago."

"I don't remember that."

"Dang, Moon, you was so drunk the night I paid you it ain't no wonder."

Moon swayed a bit more, his face darkening.

"You're telling me a lie, Primo."

Primo looked offended. "You got no call to talk that way."

Moon's temper flared like flash powder. "But you didn't pay me, Primo. You lied about it."

Primo didn't seem to know what to say. Others had overheard the argument now and were beginning to back away. Some were smiling a little, but you could tell everybody was being cautious. I only then noticed that Moon had a Remington pistol and bowie knife stuck into his pants.

Primo grinned. "Simmer down, Moon. I'll buy you a drink."

Moon thought over the offer. Finally he shook his head. "Nope, nope. You're trying to cheat me again. I'm going to have to stick you."

Primo laughed nervously and looked around at the others, waiting for them to laugh too, to verify that all this really was just a joke.

Moon pulled out his knife and stuck it into Primo's side.

CHAPTER EIGHT

Primo looked at Moon, bewildered. "Why'd you do that, Moon?"

The drunk looked at the bloody knife in his hand and the red flow coming out of Primo. His face went white and he started shaking.

"Primo, I'm sorry. I shouldn't have done that. . . . Quit bleeding, please quit. I'm sorry."

Primo slumped back against the bar. "No harm done," he said. He smiled a ghastly smile, then collapsed.

I knelt beside him. Primo's eyes were half shut. Moon started crying like a dropped baby.

"Primo, we'll get you taken care of," I said. "Don't fret." But my own heart was pounding out of my chest. I couldn't yet tell how badly he was cut.

And I didn't get a chance to check. Others pushed in then, shoving me away. I quickly saw, though, that these were people who cared about Primo and were more capable of helping him.

The barkeep came around the end of the bar with a rag. He opened Primo's shirt and pushed the rag against the ugly gash, which made Primo wince terribly, for the cloth was soaked in whiskey. Two other men held Primo still while the barkeep bathed the wound.

The woman on the stage was giving out some sort of banter about people keeping their heads, but nobody was listening to her.

"Moon, we ought to string you up!" someone said.

"I don't deny it," Moon responded through his weeping. "But I truly would appreciate it if you didn't."

The front door opened and a stocky, broad-faced man with a cigar butt in his mouth walked in. The crowd moved aside to let him pass, and I figured he was either some kind of law or a doctor.

He knelt beside Primo. "You going to make it, old friend?"

Primo, amazingly, grinned a little. "I'll do my best, Charlie."

"Good." The man, still crouching, swiveled his head and looked at the crowd. "Who did this?"

"I did," Moon said. "I was drunk and mad and foolish. He owed me thirty dollars."

"I already paid him," Primo murmured. "But I ain't mad about it."

I was beginning to see why people were so fond of Primo. You could call him a cheat and a liar and stick him with a bowie knife and he'd still stick up for you.

"I'll have to arrest you, Moon," the man said. I would hear later that he was Charlie Bassett, marshal of Dodge and former sheriff of Ford County.

"Anybody gone for the doc?" he asked.

About an hour later, Primo had been patched up and Moon Price had been hauled off to the city jail. The doctor, named McCarty just like the late U.S. marshal Primo had told me about, came over and talked to me.

"Somebody said you were with Primo."

"Yes."

"Staying at his place?"

"Well, I suppose I am."

He gave me quick instructions: "Make sure he keeps still at least a day or two; he doesn't need to infect that wound. It's minor, but he shouldn't ignore it, though he probably will." He dug into a leather bag and handed me a bottle. "Have him smear some of this on the cut two, three times a day. Keep the wound clean. I'll check in on him tomorrow or the next day. You need me, you come to my shop; it's at the intersection of Front and Second. What's your name?"

"Penn Corey."

"All right, Penn. These men here will help you get Primo home. He'll heal up fine unless he gets drunk and rampages around before that cut can knit. Primo likes to get drunk—you keep the liquor away from him."

"I'll try." I wanted to tell him that I hardly knew Primo, that I didn't know if I was really invited to stay with him, and that Primo might not want me nursemaiding him. But clearly I was stuck with the job. At least I would have a place to sleep for now.

Four men loaded Primo onto the back of a wagon and took him home, with me riding the tailgate.

Once settled into bed, Primo looked more relaxed, but I could tell the cut hurt. I thanked the men and offered them a dollar each, but they waved it off and left.

"Penn, I could sure use a swallow of whiskey to cut this pain," Primo said.

"You're already drunk, and the doctor said no alcohol for you until you're healed," I responded.

He was silent a few moments. "I suppose I might just die of this, then."

I made sure he had plenty of water and a clean chamber pot beside his bed, then I cleared a place on the floor in the front room and made a pallet from some dirty blankets I found. The room stunk badly and the bed worse, but I was so tired I fell asleep almost at once.

Seeming hundreds of bedbugs emerged from the dirt walls of the dugout. Fleas hopped about on the blankets and on me. I tossed and struggled, suffering too much to really sleep, but sleeping just deeply enough to keep me from rising—you know how that is. The night hours dragged on; every now and then I would hear a moan from Primo back in the other room.

Finally I rose to check on him; he was asleep, his brow wet with sweat. He did not seem to be in pain. I turned out of the little back room and back into the main room.

Something dark stirred, rose, loomed in the corner. I jumped back, my heart hammering. My hand fumbled for anything that could be a weapon, but then I saw that my specter was nothing but a big black dog. I hadn't seen it earlier, though in this mess it could have been asleep there since afternoon. The dog yawned, scratched, turned itself, and resettled. No wonder the place was so flea-infested. On the prairie, fleas were a problem even without dogs in the house—especially if it was a sod house or dugout—and an insuperable one with them. I started to throw the dog out, but decided it surely was Primo's and thus had more right to be in the dugout than I did.

I lay down and suffered out the rest of the night. When the welcome morning came I checked on Primo again, then clattered around about his stove to get a fire going. I made coffee and found and cleaned a skillet that had gone through several meals without a washing. That required a trip to the well outside for a bucketful of water, and on that little jaunt I got my first glimpse of Dodge by daylight.

A teamster back in Eldridge had called Dodge an ugly little town, but to me it didn't seem so. It was typical, certainly, with many unpainted buildings, lots of false fronts, and wide dirt streets lined by boardwalks. Still, it gave me a certain thrill of excitement to realize that this was Dodge City, the most talked-about and written-about city in Kansas.

Things had gone rather strangely for me here so far, I had to admit, but at least I had shelter and food. Despite my unrested, flea-bitten condition, I didn't feel like complaining at the moment. I had left my complaints behind in Eldridge.

I cooked beans and bacon. Primo groaned himself awake in the back room and fumbled for his chamber pot. After a few minutes I took his breakfast in to him.

He smiled. "Penn, you're an angel sent to care for old Primo while he's laid up," he said, reaching for the breakfast.

"Don't scald yourself on that coffee," I said. I picked up his lidded chamber pot to carry it out for emptying. It reminded me of the very unpleasant time Mrs. Halley had made me do the same for Old Halley while he was down with a fever. She said she had always been squeamish about the healthfulness of handling any slop jar but her own, which had struck me as a darned poor reason to throw the job to me. But that was typical treatment for me at the Halleys'.

As I went out, I called back, "If I'm going to sleep in here, that dog's sleeping outside. I never saw the like of fleas."

"Fine by me," Primo responded. "Ain't my dog anyway. It just sort of showed up a month ago. I been meaning to throw it out."

I had just returned the pot to beneath Primo's bed when somebody knocked on the door. I rinsed my hands in the bucket of dishwater and answered. It was Charlie Bassett, the officer who had hauled off Moon Price.

"Morning. Primo doing all right?"

"Yes sir. Come in."

Primo gave Bassett a warm, if shaky, welcome. Bassett asked what Primo wanted done about Moon.

"Nothing," Primo said.

"Nothing? He could have killed you."

"I know. But he was drunk and didn't mean no harm."

Bassett shook his head, but smiled. "Well, I figured about as much from you. If you don't want to push the matter, I won't. But he had a pistol on him, and I will at least charge him for violation of the pistol ordinance."

"But he was south of the dead line."

"Ordinance applies to the whole town, Primo. You know that. We just enforce it a little more selectively down there. But if somebody causes trouble, they can be charged just like they was north of the line."

Bassett and Primo passed the time a bit in conversation, then Bassett turned to me. "I don't think I know you, son."

"My name's Penn Corey. I'm new to Dodge."

"Friend of Primo's, huh?"

"I like to think so. He gave me a ride into Dodge on his bone wagon."

"You going to see to it he's cared for, I take it?"

"If he'll let me."

"I will. He's good as a wife," Primo said. He paused. "Most ways, at least."

Bassett grinned. "Glad you clarified that, Primo." He stood and stuck out his hand toward me. "Penn, good to meet you. You need any help from the law, call for me or Sheriff Masterson, Deputy Marshal Earp, any of us."

"I'll do it." I shook his hand.

When he was gone, I roused and kicked out the old dog with vengeful satisfaction, though doing so stirred a tremendous new cloud of fleas. I ate breakfast and then got a broom and swept up the place, washed up the old dishes, and looked in on Primo, who declared himself ready for some more sleep.

When he was snoring, I decided to walk down and explore Dodge, maybe look for work. I put a note by Primo's bed telling him what I was doing. It didn't strike me until I was well away from the dugout that Primo probably couldn't read.

I couldn't look for work dressed as I was. I had worn the same clothes for days now, and they were filthy. I had found a rip in my pants, apparently from my spill out of Mr. Littlejohn's wagon. I would have to spare at least the money for a new pair of pants and a clean shirt.

On Front Street I walked down to Wright, Beverley & Company, where I was ushered upstairs into a huge room lined with racks of pants, vests, hats, and the like. The place was well-stocked in anticipation of the coming cowboys. I bought a cheap but sturdy pair of trousers and a pale yellow shirt and donned both right there in the store. Putting my old clothes in a sack, I paid and walked back down toward a wagon shop I had seen on Front Street.

There was no work for me there, experience or not, the man in charge firmly told me. But he referred me to a new wagon works on the other side of town, over near the city livery stables on Chestnut and Railroad. Maybe I would have more luck there, he said—at least until the upstart went broke.

I walked briskly back out onto the street. A somewhat distant hammering caught my attention, and I noticed a large, obviously new house a bit farther down toward the edge of town. It was the biggest I had seen here yet, a freshly painted three-story beauty standing on a slight hill and shining in the sun. It was complete, but a one-story addition was going up on the far side; that was where the hammering came from. As I watched, a wagon rolled up the street in front of me, loaded with lumber, and went up to and around the house with a loud clatter and rumble of boards.

"There's a secret locked up in that house," a voice almost directly behind me said. It startled me badly, making me jump and feel embarrassed for it. I turned.

The strangest little man I had ever seen stood a foot from me, grinning through a wiry brown beard that spread across his upper chest. He wore an old cavalry cap and ragged clothes. His eyes gleamed in a way that immediately told that all was not right in his mind.

"Secret locked up there," he repeated, "but I know it. I've seen it." He winked and giggled. I moved away from him.

Suddenly he stopped, putting his hand to his ear. "Listen!" he said in a sharp whisper. "Hear them coming? Hear the millions of them coming?" A look of despair came over him. "Oh, do you hear the little jaws moving, eating, hear their bodies crunch beneath your feet! See them falling down like snow! They'll be the death of us, just like my Sal. I crunched them under my boots when I carried her to her grave, swept them aside with my shovel when I dug it, and still I couldn't keep them off her. They were on her when I put her away. Oh, Lord have mercy on me and poor old Sal." He began to cry.

A man had walked out of the nearby drugstore with some wrapped packages in hand. He looked at the weeping man, then at me. He must have recognized me for a newcomer—and a very bewildered one at the moment. He smiled and came over.

"Never mind him. That's just Jamey Poe," he said as if the man were not even there to hear him. "He went loco back during the hopper invasion in '74. His wife died during it—he buried her himself. Ever since then he's heard the locusts coming back. They're always just over the horizon, and every time a cloud comes up he sees it as a hopper cloud. They call him the Locust Man. He's right pitiful, huh?" The man's grin made his last sentence incongruous.

The Locust Man had calmed himself now. He dabbed his tears on his sleeve, then pointed again at the new house. "Secret hidden away," he said. He turned and walked down the street. A few yards down, he wiped his eyes again, straightened his shoulders, and began whistling.

The man with the parcels laughed and shook his head. "Jamey'll go to his grave thinking about locusts," he said. "You know that people have seen him catching grasshoppers and eating them alive?"

I wasn't enjoying this subject, so I shifted it. Pointing toward the new house, I said, "Whose place is that?"

"Why, that's the Fain house. The main part went up last fall. They started adding to it as soon as the weather warmed this year. You heard of Nigel Fain, ain't you?"

"No."

"You never heard of Nigel Fain, the man who built half the buildings in every city back east, and could buy the other half if he wanted? I thought everybody had heard of him." He looked at me for a moment as if I were about as pitiful as the Locust Man. "Let me tell you, he's a strange breed of bird. He's a cripple, for one thing. You hardly ever see him, and when you do he's got little to say. He won't take part in anything going on in town. What was Jamey saying about him, anyway?"

"Something about a secret locked in there. Something he's seen."

"Huh. Well, I don't doubt it. Old Jamey's been known to climb onto roofs and peep in windows. It lands him in the jail now and again. He's probably looked in every room in Fain's house. Takes all kinds, don't it." The man touched his hat. "Well, I'll see you around."

"Yeah."

I crossed town and found first the livery stables, then the new wagon shop. Moving around inside was a man about forty, with a pleasant face and slightly thinning brown hair. I walked in and he called a hello and came over, wiping sawdust from his hands. He had been building a wagon, and from its looks, a good one. Above the door swung a sign that read JOHNSON'S WAGON SHOP.

The man introduced himself as Dan Johnson. He was friendly and open in manner, and made a good impression right off. I gave him my false name and said I was an experienced wagon man needing work. He was amiable but hesitant. He rubbed his hand over his chin. "Penn, this is a new business, not real established just yet. I don't have the income to offer anything permanent. But I do need a hand momentarily—somebody who knows what he's doing."

"Sounds like me."

"I think maybe it does. But I like to know more about a man before I take him on."

"Let me work with you a day," I offered. "If you aren't satisfied, don't pay me a cent. If you are, pay what you think is fair." It wasn't much of a deal I was cutting, but I needed what work I could find, even temporary. If he liked me, maybe he would find a way to give me permanent employment, or at least a good reference.

He rubbed his chin again. "Can you work today?"

"I can, if you can give me an hour or so." I told him about Primo and his injury, and how I'd need to get back to prepare him some food to last the rest of the day and see that he was getting by.

He nodded. "Okay, Penn. I'll look for you back in an hour, and we'll see how you work out. I hope you work out well, because I'm on a job I want done right. See this wagon here? I'm building it for somebody who could send me a lot of work, if he likes it. I've been giving the job a lot of extra attention, but that's putting me behind on some repair jobs. Like one I got just last night—a medicine show wagon that cracked a wheel coming into town."

I paused. "May I see it?"

"Sure—but it's just your typical show wagon." He led me around back.

It was Mr. Littlejohn's wagon, all right. The front left wheel was badly cracked.

"I've seen this wagon," I said. "This medicine show was in Eldridge not long ago."

"Eldridge. Ain't that where the girl was buried and came back to life or something the other day?"

I smiled. Dixie's story was growing in the telling. "Something like that," I said. "I'll see you in about an hour. And thanks." I shook his hand.

Out on the street, the sun was bright and the day was growing hot. I headed back to Primo's dugout.

CHAPTER NINE

When I got back, Primo was up and about, against doctor's orders, and from his manner I suspected he had been pulling on a bottle while I was gone. He wasn't really drunk, just warmed up and happy. He probably had liquor stashed all about the dugout.

"Glad to hear about your work," he said after I filled him in. "There's times I hanker for a real job— but them times are rare and short in duration. I'm happier just lazying around, picking up bones and the like. Getting set right now to head out again."

"You'd best wait until that wound knits up."

"Dang, Penn, I ain't leaving until tomorrow, and I can heal as good on the prairie as I can lying here in that bed, waiting to sprout roots. Besides, them buffalo bones won't last forever. Got to get them while they're still there."

I knew better than to argue, but I did have him put on some of the medicine the doctor had given. After making sure he had food, I went out the door to go back to Johnson's Wagon Shop.

"Penn," Primo called after me, "I almost forgot to tell you: This place is your place, long as you want to stay. You've been quite a help to old Primo, and besides, you can keep an eye on the place for me while I'm gone."

I thought about the bedbugs and fleas and the vermin and could almost have been tempted to say no thanks. But I did need shelter, and Primo's was at the right price—free. And the truth was, his offer was touching.

"I'm obliged," I said. "Now you go lie down for a bit."

"I'll do it," he said, smiling, and we both knew he wouldn't.

I worked the rest of the day, and though Dan Johnson had little to say, I could tell he was pleased with me. That was nice; I had never gotten even silent appreciation from Old Halley, no matter how well I did my job.

Ironically, it seemed to me, Dan had me repair the medicine show wagon wheel. I asked Dan whether he had seen the owner of the show wagon today.

"Nope. Not since early this morning, when he took out a couple of big black boxes and a bag. Looked like picture-taking truck to me."

Now that was interesting. Mr. Littlejohn really was looking for trouble: not only had he stolen Priddy's wagon, but now he was removing his goods, probably to sell for living money. I wondered if he had sold the mules, too. Priddy was bound to show up sooner or later; when he did, there would be the devil to pay for Mr. Littlejohn. Jail time or worse. But I said nothing of this to Dan, who wasn't aware I even knew the wagon's owner beyond having seen him in Eldridge.

Just before I left at closing time, Dan shook my hand. "I like your work, Penn. Come back tomorrow. I'll work you as much as I can. I just wish I was in the position to keep you working steady."

"So do I, Dan," I told him. "I like it here."

Back at Primo's that night the bedbugs and fleas were bad as before, and my sleep just as restless. Only weariness from my day's work kept me in the bed. As I lay there, a vague feeling that something was not right kept hounding me. I sensed some presence; perhaps the dog had gotten back in. I scanned the room and saw that wasn't so. But still there was something—movement . . . above me.

I rolled onto my back and looked up. I froze, suddenly very scared.

"Easy," Primo said. He stood in the door of his room. "Easy now. Just hold still. . . ."

The blast of his shotgun was so loud it seemed it would buckle the walls of the dugout. A big, thick, Kansas variety rattlesnake that had been swinging head-down from the rafter above me spasmed and fell, the head now just a mangle. The fat body twitched and writhed for a moment on my face and neck, and I batted it off, so stunned I couldn't make a sound.

Primo walked over and picked up the snake. His

shotgun still smoked in his hand. Bird shot had peppered the wall beside me.

"That's the biggest to crawl in here yet," he said. "Good thing I heard him moving up there. You kind of develop an ear for that, living in a dugout. Did I give you a scare?"

"No. Of course not." It was all I could do to choke out the words.

"Good." He held up the limp form. "We'll skin this one and put it up on the wall with the others."

He took his snake and went back to bed. In a few moments I heard him snoring.

But for me, further sleep anytime soon was out of the question. I rose and lit a lamp; I didn't even want to set my foot down in the dark here anymore. The snakeskins tacked to the wall kept drawing my eye. Had all of those been killed inside this dugout? Probably. Dugouts and sod houses were notorious for attracting big Kansas rattlers.

I went to the front window and looked out, wondering if the shotgun blast would attract investigation. Sure enough, a man was coming around the dugout in a nightshirt, a rifle in hand. I went to the door and said, "It's all right. Primo shot a snake."

"That's what I told Betty it probably was," he said. "Good night." He turned and walked away. Primo's neighbors, apparently, were relatively used to shotgun blasts in the night.

I figured a walk might do me good, so I dressed, blew out the lamp, and headed out. It was very late, for not a light shone anywhere in this part of town. The night wind was pleasantly cool.

* * *

About a block down I saw a shadowed figure walking down a side street. The tall form and long hair
indicated it was Jonah Littlejohn. I had expected to
see him here in Dodge, though finding him wander-
ing the streets at this hour was a surprise. Maybe he
had been drinking again.

I called softly to him, but he didn't stop. I called
again.

Still he did not turn, but walked a little faster instead, digging his hands down into his pockets.

He surely had heard me. I was tense from my experience with the rattler and in no mood to be put off.

So I fell in behind Mr. Littlejohn, watching him
closely so as not to lose him in the shadows. He
turned and I turned; he walked faster and I walked
faster, closing the distance between us. He would
not turn or acknowledge me.

He turned another corner and I went after him
and found myself looking down an empty street. No
sign of him. I stopped, frowning, wondering how he
had evaded me.

"What have you got to say for yourself, chasing
down a man who's minding his own business?" It
was Mr. Littlejohn, standing in the mouth of an alley
beside me. "You're persistent on the trail, that much
I'll say for you."

"Why didn't you stop?" I asked, still irritated.

"I wasn't looking for company."

"Neither was I. But old friends ought at least to
speak."

"Old friends? I'm the man who sent you packing

on the prairie, remember? I hear tell that's not
what's generally thought friendly."

"But you're also the man who went looking for
me down the trail after that. I watched you from a
buffalo wallow."

"Then why didn't you show yourself?"

I shrugged. "Because more than one can be stubborn, I suppose. In any case, it came out all right. I
rode into town on a bone hunter's wagon. And I've
got a place to stay and sort of a job now, in the
wagon shop. It's temporary, but it will do for now. I
fixed your wagon wheel today, by the way."

"Good for you." Mr. Littlejohn was leaning with
one shoulder against the wall, his arms crossed before
him. I couldn't clearly see his face in the darkness,
which made it impossible to read his expression.
That, together with his long hair blowing somewhat
in the wind, lent a certain air of mystery to him. The
pistol we had found beneath the skeleton was thrust
into his belt.

I realized he needed to know one thing: "I've not
been using my real name, Mr. Littlejohn. I'm going
by Penn Corey now. I figure that's best, since I ran
off."

"Pleased to meet you, Penn Corey."

I asked him if he had been able to see to his unex-
plained business in Dodge yet.

He looked away. "Sometimes a man gets it in
mind to do a thing and then finds that for some reason he can't. Maybe I'll take care of it later. Maybe
not. I don't hanker to talk about it."

"How will you get by while you're here?"

Mr. Littlejohn chuckled. "I sold the mules—and old Winfred's camera. It I sold to one of the saloons, and told them the secret of the spirit photographs. They ought to be able to drum up some good business until they run out of plates."

"What's Priddy going to think about you selling his property?" I asked.

"Don't matter to me." He turned his shadow-masked face another direction, looking off across the street somewhere. "I don't care what happens about much of anything at the moment."

I didn't know what to make of that. For a few moments we stood there listening silently to the Kansas wind.

"Where are you staying?" I asked.

"I got me a room at the Great Western Hotel. Good victuals there."

A window rattled and popped nearby like it was jammed and someone was fighting to raise it. Finally it slid up, and a man in a white pointed nightcap stuck his head out. "You drunks go do your talking where folks aren't trying to sleep!" Then he fought the window down again.

I had turned away from Mr. Littlejohn when the window drew my attention. Now I turned back again. "He thinks we're drunks out on . . ."

I stopped, for he was gone—had vanished like one of Priddy's picture-ghosts might have done, had there really been such.

Halfway back to Primo's, I heard the muffled cry of a young woman.

I froze in place, listening, my heartbeat surging to

three times its previous speed. I couldn't tell where the cry had come from. Then I heard scuffling, a man's gruff voice, another short, feminine yell—the noise of struggle down a nearby alley.

I went down the alley and came out at the back of what appeared to be a saloon or dance hall. A window of a lighted room above lit the scene below: a girl struggling in the arms of a burly man. The back door of the building was slightly ajar, and I gathered the man had either come from there to grab the girl or was trying to pull her inside.

"Hey!" I yelled. "Let her go!"

The man had not seen me; my shout startled him. Intentionally or not, he loosened his grip sufficiently for her to break free. She darted away and around the far side of the building behind which we were.

The man glared at me. I got a clear look at his ugly, craggy brown face. "I'll carve you to the bowels for that!" he declared drunkenly as his hand went to a knife at his belt. He came toward me. There was a stack of clapboards against the back of the building; I grabbed a board and swung it at him. He ducked it. I swung again and knocked him down, then ran for my life.

It must have been a short run, but it seemed long to me. I turned this way and that, cutting up streets and behind buildings, at last reaching a dugout behind another saloon. The door was open, and I started to go in, but something moved inside and I fell back into the darkness a few feet.

A man came out, staggering, with four dripping beer bottles. He looked about, then hobbled off, leaving the door open. No sooner was he out of sight than I darted into the dugout and pulled the door closed. Its latch had been broken by the beer thief and would not click shut. I backed into the dark and knelt. My feet were in sawdust, my back against something cold, my hand on what felt like a case of bottles. This was the icehouse of one of the saloons, filled with ice cut from the Arkansas River the winter before.

I crouched there in the cold, panting. When the door opened again my heart almost stopped.

Someone else entered and shut the door. For a second I thought I had been discovered, but I realized it was the girl. She apparently was hiding for the same reason I was. I heard her gasping there in the little room. I thought of making my presence known, but knew that would probably scare a scream out of her and reveal where we were. I struggled to stifle my own breathing and my urge to move.

For a long time we crouched in that little icehouse together, though she did not know of me. She sniffed a little, quietly, but did not cry. The night became silent. We could hear the breeze through the dugout's wooden door, though not through the thick, earthen walls and roof.

The door slowly swung open. I dropped flat against the ground, and the girl did the same.

Dimly silhouetted within the frame of the door was the man with the knife. He stood there a long time, peering in. I heard the striking of a match, then a feeble yellow flicker lit the room as he held the match aloft.

I was behind several cases of beer and he could not see me from where he was. Whether the girl was safe from view I could not tell, but after a few moments I decided she was, for the man did not move or say anything.

The match went out. The man muttered in profane resignation to the fact he had lost his quarry. A moment later the door closed. I exhaled quietly in relief.

A minute passed, and the girl moved a bit. I thought then I would let her know I was there, but at that moment she rose, pushed on the door, and left at a run.

I went after her. She ran onto Second Avenue, then onto Front Street, where she turned right. I followed, keeping some distance back.

The darkness had almost made her invisible when I saw her turn and run up the hill toward the big house of Nigel Fain.

CHAPTER TEN

Primo hitched up his wagon and pulled out the next morning. I waved him off and headed for work, missing him even before he was fully out of sight.

Shortly before noon, a cane-carrying man in a derby and matching dark suit with a gold watch chain across the vest walked into the wagon shop. He touched his derby brim, nodded politely, and said good morning to Dan and me. He sported a neatly trimmed mustache and had two of the most intense eyes I had ever seen.

"What can I do for you, sheriff?" Dan asked. I realized the man was Sheriff Bat Masterson.

"I'm looking for a Mr. Corey," he said. About ten seconds later, after my heart started beating again, I said, "That's me."

Masterson, still smiling that polite, calm smile, asked if I would accompany him to the courthouse a block or so up. I dusted off my hands and went.

I was a little surprised to see Masterson, much less

be sought out by him, for Dan had said Masterson had been out of town a lot this year. First he had gone to Fort Leavenworth to pick up a handful of Indians who were to go on trial later for participation in the Dull Knife raids of the previous fall. After that he had been called up to form a sort of militia to keep the peace in a railroad war in Colorado.

Apparently, though, Masterson wasn't too busy to round up young runaways, which was how I perceived the situation at the moment. I was surprised Old Halley had cared enough to put out the word about me.

Masterson said nothing as we walked together. He limped slightly and used his cane to steady himself. Despite his limp, he was a straight-spined, dignified man whom I found thoroughly intimidating.

When we arrived, the Dull Knife raiders were sunning themselves on the front steps of the courthouse under the oversight of the jailer, whom Masterson greeted with another touch to the derby and a nod.

The Indians looked like someone had taken an eraser and rubbed out their souls. They blankly watched Masterson and me ascend the steps. It was hard to comprehend that only a few months before, these men supposedly had been among raiders who had killed several people, raped several women, and run off or stolen livestock all over western Kansas.

When we walked into Masterson's office, Charlie Bassett was seated on the desk, and in a chair beside him sat Mr. Littlejohn, looking dejected.

Now I wasn't at all sure what was going on.

"Mr. Littlejohn, have we brought you the right fellow?" Masterson asked.

Mr. Littlejohn nodded.

"Good." Masterson turned to me. "Mr. Corey, don't be alarmed. We merely need you to give us a few facts. Marshal Bassett here arrested Mr. Littlejohn early this morning after he got rather . . . uppity when faced with a few questions. Marshal Bassett had noticed Mr. Littlejohn carrying a pistol in town, north of the dead line. Then he saw it was not just any pistol . . . Charlie, where is that Colt?"

Bassett produced from behind him the 1860 Army Colt Mr. Littlejohn and I had found beneath the skeleton east of Dodge.

"Does that weapon look familiar to you, Mr. Corey?" Masterson asked.

"Yes sir," I said. "We found that pistol out on the prairie."

"We?"

"Mr. Littlejohn and I."

"Where did you find it, exactly?"

"I couldn't tell you the exact spot at the moment, but it was beside a rock—underneath a dead man."

Masterson nodded. "I see. Anything else on the dead man?"

"No. No sign as to who he was."

"Thank you, Mr. Corey." Masterson motioned to Bassett and they walked to the corner of the room. There they put their heads together and talked quietly. I slipped over to Mr. Littlejohn.

"What's the problem here?" I whispered, and Masterson immediately called me down.

"Please refrain from talking between yourselves for the moment, friends."

I went to a chair across the room and didn't say another word. But I thought I had it figured out: I had been brought in simply to verify Mr. Littlejohn's story. He obviously had told them about me, which I wasn't happy about, but apparently had used my false name, which I did appreciate.

Masterson and Bassett glanced back at us occasionally as they talked. In the meantime, I heard the jailer bringing the Indians back into the jail below, a dark stone dungeon locals called the "lime kiln."

The two peace officers came back to their original spots. Masterson fastened those intense eyes on me and smiled again.

"Mr. Corey, where did you come from?"

My throat became a sandy desert. "Eldridge, sir."

"You traveled from there with Mr. Littlejohn?"

"Part of the way. Then he threw me off . . . What I mean is, I got off and walked a bit, then rode in the rest of the way on Primo Smith's bone wagon."

Bassett came to life then. "Now I remember—you were with Primo at the Lady Gay, and at his dugout."

"Yes sir."

"Why did you come to Dodge?" Masterson asked.

"Just to come," I said. I had no better answer handy.

"How old are you?"

"Twenty." I hoped he would believe it. Masterson's eyes told me he didn't. But he didn't pursue it.

"Thank you, Mr. Corey," he said. "You may go now."

"Thanks," I said. I turned toward the door, but curiosity made me turn again.

"May I ask something, Sheriff? Why were you so interested in that Colt we found?"

"It's a familiar pistol to Charlie and me, recognizable from that brass swivel ring," he said. "It belonged to a fellow who lived in Dodge from time to time and gave us peace officers our share of headaches. He always loved that pistol. He left Dodge in the dead of winter, on the run—he had riled a few of his ilk some way or another. I looked for him to come back, but he never did. When we saw that pistol, frankly, we thought maybe Mr. Littlejohn had murdered him."

"I can vouch he didn't," I said.

"You already have, through what you told us," Masterson said. "I think it's likely the weather was what killed Emo. That was his name—Emo Moles. Emo wasn't much of a loss to this world, though he did play a decent piano when he was sober."

That night I went looking for Mr. Littlejohn at the Great Western, but he was not there. I decided to check the saloons.

The streets were lively tonight; the town was filling with those who came in advance of the herds and cowboys—gamblers, showmen, drummers, prostitutes. Across the Santa Fe tracks, the famous entertainer Eddie Foy had returned to the Lady Gay Dance Hall, where he had performed the previous summer. His return had been the talk of Dodge today.

I passed the Long Branch, which along with the

Occident, the Old House, and a few other saloons along Front Street, had the reputation of being a relatively genteel establishment. It was north of the dead line, so the law against carrying weapons was enforced there. Prostitutes and rowdies were not tolerated, and even dancing was forbidden.

Not that such strictness always managed to keep the peace. It was in the Long Branch just a short while back, according to Dan Johnson, that a gambler called Cock-Eyed Frank Loving had used a .44 Remington to gun down a freighter named Richardson in a brawl over a woman. Primo had made mention of the fight to me already, but Dan gave more details—and to hear him describe it, it was a miracle that several innocent people hadn't taken bullets, for the two combatants had circled the room, firing point-blank at each other. Richardson finally fell, and Loving was taken into the custody of Charlie Bassett. A brief hearing resulted in a ruling that Loving had shot in self-defense, and he had gone free.

All this I thought about as I walked into the long, rather narrow building. It was packed. Music drifted up from a five-piece band playing in the rear. The bar was long and painted white, and behind it hung a big mirror topped by a set of horns off a Texas longhorn. Chandeliers hung from a high ceiling.

Two drunks jostled past me and out the door. I let them by, then walked toward the bar.

Mr. Littlejohn stood out in all crowds, this one included. He was leaning over the bar with a glass of beer in his hand. His long hair was tucked up behind his ears and was a little damp with sweat. I walked toward him.

"I see those peace officers didn't send you to Leavenworth," I said.

He gave me a sidewise glance and took a sip of his beer. "Nope."

"They let you keep the pistol?"

"Yep."

"You got it on you?"

"Wouldn't tell if I did."

I nodded. "Well, I can tell when a man doesn't want company. I just came in to tell you I appreciated you not giving my real last name to those peace officers. Having said it, I'll leave you be." I turned away.

He touched my shoulder. "Don't be that way. Come here and have a drink with me."

"I don't want a drink."

"You're getting one anyway." He called the bartender over and bought me a beer.

Mr. Littlejohn took a swallow of his own beer. "Quite a town, don't you think?"

"Yeah. How long you plan to stay?" I was wondering again about his unfinished business, but didn't want to ask directly.

"Until I make up my mind what I want to do."

"You aren't ever going to tell me what you came for, are you?"

"Doubt I will." He took another sip. "Let's just say there's somebody here I need to make a call on."

At that moment a man stood abruptly at a table at the end of the room, yelled something at another man, who was rising just across from him, then threw himself bodily across the table. A general shout rose; men backed away from the fighters, taking their drinks with them. You could tell who held the best poker hands; they were the ones who kept their cards as well as their drinks.

The fighters writhed atop the table for a moment, then crashed to the floor and rolled, pushing chairs out of their way as they did. One bounded up, and my heart almost exited by way of my throat when I saw he had a knife.

Mr. Littlejohn saw it too and grabbed the man's uplifted arm, thus saving the intended victim below from a stab. With a single twist Mr. Littlejohn cracked the man's wrist and the knife fell; Mr. Littlejohn kicked it into the corner.

"You broke my wrist!" the man said, so awed he almost sounded reverent. But simultaneously he reached under his jacket with his good hand.

Mr. Littlejohn kicked him in the abdomen. The man went down so hard he banged his head on the edge of a table during his descent and split the skin.

The man who would have been stabbed got up and ran out without so much as a word of thanks to Mr. Littlejohn.

A drunk waded in toward Mr. Littlejohn, swearing at him. He probably was a friend or relative of the first unfortunate. Mr. Littlejohn put a fist into this one's face.

At that point a general fight was on. Several men apparently wanted a taste of Mr. Littlejohn's medicine themselves, and he served it up much more enthusiastically than he ever had bottles of Dr. Demorest's Radical Purge. Man after man fell beneath his fists. At least two actually wound up flying over the bar.

The confusion grew. A big hand came down on my shoulder. Mr. Littlejohn grinned.

"Come on," he said. "Let's get out of here."

Together we headed for the door. In a moment the law would be here, and Masterson and Bassett would not be merciful twice in one day to Mr. Littlejohn and me.

We loped down the boardwalk. We looked at each other and laughed. I had not seen Mr. Littlejohn laugh before.

"Nothing like a good healthy round or two to put a man at ease," he said. "And this one may be just the advertisement I need. Let's head down a ways and see."

I wasn't sure what he was talking about, but I had my suspicions.

They were confirmed minutes later.

Mr. Littlejohn and I had gone down to the Old House saloon and found a table. He ordered two more beers. We talked over the fight a bit. Mr. Littlejohn kept watching the door, as if he expected someone.

A couple of minutes later, two men came in, looked around the place, and headed straight for us.

"This may be what I'm looking for right now," Mr. Littlejohn said sidewise.

The men were smiling and friendly. One sat

down uninvited at our table, and the other stood by, grinning.

"My name's R. B. Polk," the seated fellow said. "They tell me your name is Littlejohn."

"Who's 'they,' and why are they talking about me?"

Polk leaned back in his chair and spread his arms expansively. "Half the town's talking about you at the moment, Mr. Littlejohn. You made quite a show in the Long Branch."

"Just trying to help keep a fellow human being alive. Otherwise I wouldn't have gotten into it."

"Well, it was a noble gesture and all that, but your nobility's not what brings me. I'm more interested in your muscle. Tell me—do you sometimes fight for sport?"

Mr. Littlejohn took a swallow of beer. "I've been known to. For the right money, that is."

Polk said, "So I thought. You have a fighter's style and bearing. I believe you could top any man thrown against you. Are you employed anywhere?"

"Not at the moment."

"Well, then! You are now. To prove my good faith, let me show you this. . . ."

Polk produced a wad of green, which he held up.

"This is yours, on the spot. All you need to do is agree to fight for me. One fight. I've set up and promoted many a bout, my good fellow, and I know how to do it to maximum advantage. Those Texas drovers come in thirsting for some good slugology, as the papers here call it.

"But don't let me push your decision. Sleep on it,

and I'll look you up tomorrow and put this cash in your hand—if you give a positive answer. Where can I find you?"

Mr. Littlejohn shook his head. "You won't find me; I'll find you."

Polk smiled. "You are a careful man. Very well. Look for me in the Dodge House, room twenty-one. I'll expect you in the morning." He grabbed Mr. Littlejohn's hand and shook it. "To partnership and profit," he said.

When they were gone, I sat there feeling glad, for once, that I was a rather spare and thin fellow. It seemed to me that it would be rather depressing, being sought out for fights all the time. But seemingly it caused Mr. Littlejohn no distress. In fact, he seemed happy at the moment.

But as time went by and more beers went down his throat, his conversation fell off and he descended into a silent, pensive brood. Beginning to feel in his way once more, I told him good night and started back to the dugout, wondering what nagged at him so. As I went out the saloon door a man walked in and announced loudly that the first herds would reach the south bank of the Arkansas tomorrow.

A general cheer went up. The 1879 cattle season was about to descend on Dodge City.

CHAPTER ELEVEN

In the morning, right after the first herds reached the southern bank of the river, Dan asked me to deliver the wagon he had been building. When he told me the recipient was Nigel Fain, I perked up, gladdened by the prospect of seeing the house up close—and maybe the girl, too. I had thought about her much since the incident in the alley and the icehouse.

South of the Santa Fe tracks, the open prairie teemed with longhorns. The wiry animals, thinned and muscled from the long drive from Texas, grazed and rested under the supervision of riders.

Cowboys already roamed the town, many about my age or just a little older. The barber shop was doing a brisk business in baths and haircuts. Most of the cowboys were decked out in brand-new duds from Wright, Beverley & Company. The merchants, saloon keepers, gamblers, keno callers, faro dealers, and restauranteers had their brightest smiles on today.

As I approached the Fain house, a workman busy

on the newest part of the building stopped and watched me drive up. A young Chinaman carrying dirty dishwater out to dump in the back also paused and eyed me. My impression was that visitors did not come here often and were a curiosity.

I parked, climbed down, and went to the front door. The knock echoed back through the big building. In a few moments the door opened and the same Chinaman I had seen at the back motioned me in. I entered and slipped off my hat.

"I've got a wagon for Mr. Fain," I said. "And a copy of his bill that I can leave—"

A flurry of motion in a hallway nearby cut me off. "It's him!" a voice said. "He's the one!" I turned just in time to see the girl dart from the hall and across the room toward two heavy oak doors at the far end. A side door opened first, though, and a tall man in a business suit came out and caught her before she reached the double doors.

"He's busy, dear," the man said. "What's the stir?"

She pointed back at me again. The Chinaman had stepped aside and was looking at me like I was a great dignitary. The tall man gave me an intense once-over as well and whispered back and forth with the girl. He nodded and strode toward me.

"Good morning," he said. "I am Theodore Crarie, Mr. Fain's secretary and assistant. Won't you have a seat over here?"

"Is there a problem?" I asked.

"No indeed. Quite the opposite. I think Mr. Fain may wish to see you. You are . . ."

"Penn Corey. I'm with Dan Johnson's wagon shop."

"Indeed, indeed. Come inside, young sir."

I walked in and sat down. The girl was half-hidden in the corner of the room, watching me intently, a little smile on her lips. I wished I could see her more clearly. I felt her gaze on me. Crarie left me and went to the big double doors, knocked, then entered. A few moments later he came out.

"Mr. Corey—this way, please."

The room behind the doors was plush. Very old paintings in gilded frames hung on the walls, which themselves were an ornate blend of varnished wainscot and columns and intricately patterned paper. A rich purplish carpet on the floor looked deep enough to swallow a man like quicksand. I stepped out onto it as the doors closed behind me, shutting me in. Crarie had not entered with me.

At the end of the room was a huge polished desk, and behind it a man in a tall chair. He was about fifty, with no hair on the top but thick, peppery bushes around the ears. He wore very small wire-rimmed spectacles on his largish nose. His complexion was naturally rosy, but he looked like a man who spent most of his time indoors. He wore a business suit. When he pushed back in the chair, I realized it was a wheelchair.

"Hello, Mr. Corey," he said in a clear, soft voice as he rolled his chair around the desk and toward me. His legs were thin sticks beneath his trousers. He reached out his right hand to shake mine. "I am Nigel Fain."

"Pleased, sir." Holding up the bill, I said, "I just came to deliver your wagon."

He took the bill and tossed it onto the desk behind him without looking at it. "Yes. But forget the wagon for now. It is my understanding you were of help to my daughter."

"I recently found a young lady in an unpleasant situation, if that's what you mean," I said. "I believe it was the young lady outside."

"Melanie, my daughter," Fain said. "A young girl sometimes prone to risks and trouble, just like her . . ." He stopped a moment, then continued. "A girl thoughtless enough to leave her home unannounced and wander through streets filled with saloons and brothels in the middle of the night. If not for you, she might have been badly hurt . . . or humiliated. She told about it all when she came running home."

"I really didn't do anything more than show up at the right time," I said.

"It was enough. Any help is a blessing in this hellish town."

I wondered why a man who hated a town so would move into it. Fain surely had enough wealth to live where he pleased.

"At any rate, there is at least one good man in Dodge—you've shown that," he said. "I fully intend to reward you."

"No need for that," I said. All the same, I welcomed the prospect.

"There is the need, in my opinion." He rolled over to a safe against the wall, cranked the knob, and opened it. "Business is difficult in a town without a bank," he noted as he dug inside the safe and shuffled paper. He wheeled and glided back to me, extending an envelope.

"This is not payment for the wagon, but strictly reward for you. Take it with my thanks, Mr. Corey. As for the bill, Mr. Crarie will issue payment at the end of the week. If we are pleased with the work there will be more business to come."

"Thank you, sir," I said. The envelope felt well stuffed. "I don't feel I should take this."

"Take it, take it. Believe me, I can afford to pay those who do me a good turn. And if you ever need help of any kind, any kind at all, all you need do is show up at my door. I'm serious about that. If you need me, I'm here to help."

"Thank you," I said.

Crarie stood outside the door like a guardian. He smiled, nodded, and waved me toward the front door. I put on my hat and walked out.

The girl was on the porch. Without a word she darted to me, threw her arms around me, kissed me, then turned and ran inside.

I walked back toward the wagon shop in a near-daze, the kiss still burning wonderfully on my cheek, and stepped into an alley to look into my envelope.

A hundred dollars. I stared at it, disbelieving.

There was no particular hurry to get back to the wagon shop; Dan had already told me that, once the Fain wagon was delivered, there would be no more work for me for a while. Not that I needed work now. It was ironic that just as my prospects had appeared to be thinning, my wallet had suddenly grown fat.

I put the envelope into my pocket and rounded a corner. I had to stifle a yell when I came face to face with Jamey, the Locust Man.

"I seen you come from the secret place," he said, grinning at me about five inches from my face. "Did you see the secret? Did you see what hides there?"

"I didn't see anything," I said. "I just delivered a wagon."

"You got to climb to see secrets," he said. "Over the rooftops, along the windows. That's what I do. I look in windows and find secrets. There's much sin in this town. The plague of locusts will come again. Keep your ears open! Listen for the coming of the living cloud!"

Unexpectedly, he leaped straight up, grabbed the edge of the roof overhang on the one-story building beside us, and swung himself up. He crouched up there, perched like a squirrel, and then scampered off over the peak and out of sight.

I had read once that Dodge was full of strange characters, but the Locust Man surely was the strangest I expected to see. Also the most nimble.

I went up to the dugout and hid my money in a jar. It would be safe there; no thief would figure to find anything of value in a hole like this.

I kept a few dollars in my pocket, which made me feel rich and ready to celebrate. Had Primo been here I would have offered him a meal. As it was, I decided to share my good fortune with Mr. Littlejohn.

I walked down Third Avenue, crossed Front Street and the dead line, then headed for the Great Western. Mr. Littlejohn's wagon was parked outside it. The Great Western was quite a building. The chief competitor of the Dodge House, it was a homey place that was known for its outstanding suppers of wild game.

I found Mr. Littlejohn's room, and him in it. He was shaving in a basin in the corner and looked solemn indeed. Maybe he was hungover from beer drinking last night. Whatever the reason, he seemed reluctant to let me in, and his manner hinted to me of the way he was just before we parted ways on the trail to Dodge.

"Did you set up your fight?" I asked by way of making conversation.

"I did." He crooked his arm, twisted up his mouth, and shaved carefully under his lower lip.

"Where's it going to be?"

"Behind Boot Hill. Tomorrow night, late."

"Figure to make good money?"

"Wouldn't do it if I didn't." He looked at me with slight irritation. "What's the point of all the questions?"

"Nothing. Just making conversation." His somber bearing was a bit intimidating, and I wondered if I should bother asking him to share a meal.

He went back to shaving and I sat there in silence for a while, feeling in the way. "Where did you learn to fight?" I asked.

He looked at me darkly and did not answer. I tugged at the brim of my hat in my hands. "Not my business, I suppose."

"Not really, no."

I began to feel irritation of my own. "Look, there's no call for you to act so ill. I came to invite you to a meal."

He turned, a bit surprised. "Since when did you get money enough to ask a man to a meal? Or do you plan to fry up some lizards you caught?" He laughed at his own joke.

"A man can sometimes run into some money in ways other than trouncing some cowboy behind Boot Hill," I returned.

Mr. Littlejohn frowned. "Did you steal something?"

"I'm no thief. You're the wagon-taker, remember?" I meant the comment lightly, but he didn't appear to take it so.

"So where will this meal be?"

"Pick your restaurant. I got enough money. When I took the wagon up to Mr. Fain, he—"

I was not ready for the way Mr. Littlejohn wheeled on me. His face was stormy with unexpected anger.

"Don't say that name in my presence. Don't breathe it, don't think it."

I stood there with my mouth open, utterly taken aback.

"I'm sorry," I said. "I'll say nothing more about it." Nor about providing Mr. Littlejohn a meal, for he obviously was in no mood for one.

Mr. Littlejohn's anger quickly abated, and he looked a bit embarrassed.

"Forget all this," he said. "I really didn't mean to . . . Just forget it." He broke off, then spoke more brightly. "I'll tell you what—there is something you can do for me."

Why I should want to do something for him after

his outburst at me wasn't at all clear, but I heard him out.

"The man I'm to fight—his name is Crampton and he's with a herd from Texas run by an outfit called the Shooting Iron. I can't very well go take a look at him myself, but I'd appreciate it if you would. I like to know the kind of man I'm to face."

"How will I know him?"

"Ask somebody. Most likely whoever it is will be the biggest man there. I want to know how big. Whether it's fat or muscle. What kind of reputation he's got. Talk around in the background with some folks, but don't let on why."

I agreed, said goodbye, and left him. Alone I ate the meal I had intended to share and, because I was alone, had an extra piece of pie for dessert. Then I walked toward the plains south of the Arkansas.

I crossed the little bridge over Hog Creek and the big one over the river. Before me stretched an unending plain covered with longhorns. Amid the brown milling herds were cowboys on horseback, chuckwagons, supply wagons, and brightly dressed drummers from town hawking goods. Smoke rose from cookfires, sending white plumes to the wide blue sky. Far out across the way I saw another herd arriving.

Nearly every face I saw was caked in trail dust, but bright with anticipation. Cowboys coming in off a drive were like sailors reaching port after a long voyage. They were ready for carousing.

I called to a young cowboy a little younger than I and he rode over on his claybank mare.

"I'm looking for the Shooting Iron outfit. You seen them?"

"Right there, yonder." He pointed southwest.

I thanked him and headed that way. Nearby I noticed four cowboys in brand-new clothing showing something to three others who still wore their dirty trail garb. The four obviously had already been to town, bathed, and bought new duds; the others must have been new arrivals. All of them were gazing intently at what I now saw was a photograph.

One of the local cyprians in a scandalous pose, I figured. But then I heard one of them saying, "It's amazing! I swear she wasn't there with me. And look at them wings she's got!" My suspicions aroused, I walked around the back of the group and glanced over. Sure enough, the photograph was one from Priddy's old camera. Its subject was one of the cleaned-up cowboys before me, and floating off to the side was the same angel that had turned up in Dixie Trimble's photograph. I almost laughed. Whatever saloon had bought the camera from Mr. Littlejohn would probably do good business among the cowboys as word of this got out.

I walked on past and shortly thereafter located what I was sure was the Shooting Iron outfit. Among the group was a man about the height of Mr. Littlejohn but much heavier. I asked a passerby if that was Crampton, and he verified it was.

"Meanest old grizzly between the Rockies and the Mississippi," he added.

I feared for Mr. Littlejohn; this Crampton looked like he could defeat three Gene Garfields without even breaking into a sweat.

"Crampton's going to fight outside town tomorrow night," the man said. "You ought to come see it. Crampton fights mean. Killed another fighter in Laredo once."

After eyeing Crampton awhile longer, I went back to the Great Western and reported to Mr. Littlejohn.

"This man could kill you," I said. "He's already killed one fighter."

"I guarantee you I've faced worse."

"Well, if you go through with it, I think I'll skip watching this fight. I don't take a cotton to seeing you get beat to death."

"Suit yourself. But take my advice: If you do come, bet on me."

At that moment an uncomfortable, almost prophetic feeling swept over me, as unexpected as a burst of sickness when you've been feeling well. It was a dark, foreboding dread that went beyond mere concern about this Crampton fellow. *Don't go through with this fight*, I wanted to say to Mr. Littlejohn. *Things are about to go badly for you, badly in a big way—I don't know how I know it, but I do.*

That thought was so unnerving that I wheeled and walked out of Mr. Littlejohn's room without even a goodbye. When I was down the hall I heard him shut the door.

CHAPTER TWELVE

The night of the fight came, and the wind was up, kicking dust into clouds that swept along the streets and rattled against the windows. Newly arrived cowboys walked Front Street or crossed the Santa Fe tracks to the wilder dives and dance halls on the other side. I saw Deputy Marshal Wyatt Earp hauling in a drunk toward the city jail, a dismal little building just across the railroad tracks from the Lone Star Saloon. The jail was in the lower part of a building built of boards laid flat and pegged together; above it were the city offices. The drunk's nose was bloody, and if he had resisted Earp's arrest before, he did not now.

No sooner had Earp deposited his prisoner than a series of shots, intermixed with exultant whoops, rang out from a band of rowdy horsemen racing south over the Arkansas River bridge. Earp took off in that direction in long strides.

I looked west, and in the darkness at that end of

Front Street I saw the movement of a familiar female form—a skirt dancing like a wraith's sheet, barely visible.

I went toward her. She had slipped between two buildings. Above and across from there, loomed the tall house of Nigel Fain. Light shone from one high window.

A blowing cloud of grit swirled around me and stung my face. I put my hand on my hat and looked around. "Where are you?"

A slight rustle, a movement in the dark. I thought I picked up a wind-torn fragment of feminine laughter.

I went toward the spot from which it had come, but she was not there. Another laugh now, from a different place. I smiled. This was a game. I again chased the sound, and again did not find her.

I squinted into the breeze. "All right—suit yourself!" I leaned against a wall and crossed my arms over my chest, waiting.

Her laugh this time was closer. I saw her as my eyes grew more accustomed to the dark. She was about fifteen feet from me, posed almost as I was, her back against a wall and her arms folded.

"Talk to me," she said, almost teasingly. "I want to hear your voice."

"Does your father know you're roaming the streets again?" I asked.

"Why should he know? Am I his prisoner?" Her voice was melodic. Her dark hair blended with the shadows of the wall against which she leaned. Her dress also was dark; she was a girl of shadows.

"I don't know. Are you?" I asked.

Now her tone became less playful. "Yes . . . I am. And that house is my jail."

I took a step toward her. "Is that so bad? There's not a nicer place in all Dodge. Where I stay, snakes sometimes drop from the ceiling."

"There are worse things than snakes," she said.

"Yes," I responded. "Like drunks who grab you from alleyways. Didn't your last trip onto the streets put any fear into you?"

"You sound like Father. I'm not a fearful person. Not of much, at least."

She suddenly came toward me. "Come with me," she said, her hand extended. I took it. A cold wind tore through the alley to strike us, yet I felt warm.

She led me across the dark street and the railroad tracks. To our left was noise and music and voices, and to our right the silent flatlands. The Fain house stood before us.

We walked together up the hill, and she led me to the back of the house. Here the wind was steady, and she was so close it blew her hair against my face. The lone, upper-level light inside the house made a window glare down on us like a cyclop's eye. It was covered by a white curtain.

We sat on the ground together. A shadow passed over the lighted window, and I felt her tense beside me.

"Your father?" I asked.

"No. No. But don't talk of that. Tell me where you have been. Have you been to places far away?"

I shook my head. "No. To the mountains in Colorado is the farthest. I've mostly just been in Kansas. I've never had the means to travel much. But I would think you have, with your father's wealth."

"I've moved, but it's the same everywhere. All places seem the same when you aren't the one who chose to go there. I want to go very far away, so far no one can find me or tie me down. I want to live in a big city and go where I want to go, with no one to control me."

"I've been told your father has built big cities."

"I don't want his cities."

I asked her why her family had come to Dodge. The shadow passed the window again.

"Because of her," she said. "Because Father thought it would help her. Everything he does, he does for her."

"We're talking about your mother?"

"Yes. The one who holds chains around my father. And me." Her next words were whispered, spoken with a shudder. "She is so horrible, horrible."

Something in that was downright chilling, and though it made me curious, it also made me unsure whether I wanted to hear more. I looked across the distance, and my eye happened to fall on what I could see of Boot Hill. I changed the subject.

"There's a fight going on across there tonight," I said. "Hand to hand, two men."

She turned to me eagerly. "Take me there! I want to see it."

It was a surprising request. "No, Melanie. I don't think you really would. Those things can grow very ugly."

"Take me there, Penn. Please." It was the first time she had called my name.

"Well . . ." I would have loved being with her, but it did not seem appropriate to take her to the fight. Besides, I felt like I was betraying Fain's reward even by being out here right now. I knew he would want her to be inside. Not that I wanted her to go; this kind of guilt I could easily live with.

A woman's voice came from inside the house, muffled but audible. Then a crashing sound, like someone had thrown something against a wall. The voice was louder now, sounding agitated. Another light flickered on in the house a moment later. Melanie closed her eyes.

"It starts again," Melanie said. "Over and over it's the same. She'll be the death of my father."

Her reference to Fain prompted a question: "Melanie, the fight I mentioned: One of the men in it knows your father, though I don't know how. The man's name is Jonah Littlejohn, and—"

She had turned to me, wide and lips parted. She looked afraid. "He's *here?* In Dodge?" Without another word she rose and ran back to the house, opened a back door, and disappeared inside.

Slowly I walked toward Boot Hill, trying to understand the strange encounter just completed.

Melanie had left me with a mix of impressions: sadness, restlessness, beauty. Mostly beauty. She was attractive enough by daylight, but in the night she was in the element that best suited her. Maybe it subtly matched the darkness of her spirit.

In any case, already her features and form had become part of my mental furniture, and I felt it unlikely that many moments would pass henceforth when I was not devoting at least part of my thoughts to her.

I wondered what it was in her life that made her feel so imprisoned, and about the woman up in that lighted room. And why the mere name of Mr. Littlejohn had roused the response from Melanie that it had, just as mention of Melanie's father had roused a similar reaction from Mr. Littlejohn.

Preoccupied with such thoughts, I hardly noticed that I was, contrary to my earlier announced intention, heading right now for Mr. Littlejohn's fight. Perhaps it was mere distraction; perhaps it was Melanie's inexplicable interest in the fight that lured me there. Why would a young lady, probably of delicate raising, want to see such a brawl? Because such a thing was alien to the world she both lived in and despised? Perhaps it was that same attraction that led her from her house at night to walk among saloons, brothels, and gambling halls.

I climbed Boot Hill's southeast side, walking through the empty graveyard where some of the holes that had been reopened earlier this year still were empty. The former occupants of these graves now lay outside the fences of the town's new Prairie Grove Cemetery. Inside the fence were those of more dignified rank; still other dignitaries of the town, such as slain marshal Ed Masterson, were buried over in the Fort Dodge cemetery.

Before I reached the crest of the hill I heard the

sound of the fight and saw the glow of torches, reminding me of the night outside Eldridge when Mr. Littlejohn had humiliated Gene Garfield. I now saw the ring of people, mostly men, though there were also dance hall girls and cyprians there.

I moved around until I had a good position to see the status of the fight. When I did, I smiled, for Mr. Littlejohn was winning.

At the moment, he was bashing the face of the big cowboy, Crampton, whose arms flailed like two swinging smokehouse hams. Mr. Littlejohn dodged and ducked those arms, putting down a steady pounding against Crampton's wide face.

As before, Mr. Littlejohn still wore his shirt; the other man was bare-chested, glistening with sweat and blood. He howled like a puma as Mr. Littlejohn drove him steadily back. Finally Crampton collapsed. I sat on the edge of an empty grave and dangled my feet into the hole, watching what I was sure would be a short and decisive finish.

From the actions and shouts of the people below, I gathered that most had bet against Mr. Littlejohn. I could understand why. The man he was so thoroughly defeating was the obvious choice for winner, judging from appearance alone. But as I already knew, Mr. Littlejohn was not an obvious man who fell into obvious categories.

The big cowboy had arisen now; Mr. Littlejohn stepped back and let him get up. I rose and walked down the hill a little to get a closer view of the fight's impending end. Crampton could not possibly win; his nose was smashed and bloody, and he staggered on his feet. He stumbled toward Mr. Little-

john and swung, and again Mr. Littlejohn dodged
the blow and drove his fist into Crampton's chin.

The cowboy staggered back and fell at the edge of
the crowd. A man came forward as Crampton tried
to get up, and I saw who it was.

Winfred Priddy. In his hand was a rolled-up bullwhip. As Crampton rose, Priddy put the whip into
his hand.

"Here now, that's not fair!" someone shouted. But
others cheered.

I ran down the hill to the back of the crowd and
began pushing through. When I reached the edge of
the ring, Mr. Littlejohn was glaring at Priddy.
Crampton smiled through his blood and unfurled
the bullwhip; he moved it threateningly, making it
ripple like a snake.

"Lay him open!" Priddy yelled to Crampton.
"Flay the hide off him!"

"Put down that whip," Mr. Littlejohn said. "This
is a fistfight, not a whip fight."

"It's lap jacket!" someone shouted, referring to a
vicious game in which opponents whipped each
other. "Go to it, cowboy!"

"It ain't lap jacket unless they both got whips,"
somebody else protested.

Crampton cracked the whip and laughed. He advanced on Mr. Littlejohn.

I yelled, "Somebody stop this!" No one moved.
Crampton still advanced. I started to lunge out into
the ring, but strong hands gripped my shoulder and
pulled me back.

Mr. Littlejohn had, through defeating Crampton
with his fists, put himself on the bad side of most of

the people here who had bet on Crampton. There seemed to be a general thirst for Mr. Littlejohn's blood.

Crampton raised and brought down the whip. Mr. Littlejohn flinched down and missed taking it across the face; instead it ripped over his shoulders, tearing a big gash in his shirt. Blood came through.

The crowd cheered. Priddy laughed; the laugh rang on after the cheer had faded.

"No!" I shouted, struggling with whoever held me. The grip only tightened; two men wrestled me down and pinned me.

Held there, I could only twist my head and watch what was happening in the ring.

Crampton lashed Mr. Littlejohn again, then again. The sound of the whip on flesh was horrible. Mr. Littlejohn's shirt was being shredded, his shoulders and back turned to a bloody mangle. Crampton, his teeth gritted beneath his bloody lips, advanced and whipped his victim savagely. All the while Priddy was laughing and all but leaping in delight at the edge of the ring.

It went on the longest time, until Mr. Littlejohn collapsed. The spirit of the crowd changed then, and men surged in and separated Crampton from his victim. Someone wrenched the bullwhip away from Crampton and tossed it to the side of the ring, where Priddy picked it up.

The men holding me let go. I leaped up and ran into the ring to Mr. Littlejohn, who lay facedown. His back heaved with every struggling breath. His shirt was a tatter soaked in blood.

Someone came up with a torch, and light spilled onto the bare, bloodied back.

There was something wrong with the flesh there, wrong beyond being whipped raw. What was on his back didn't really look like flesh at all, but thick, ugly scars. Burn scars, very bad ones. His shoulders, the small of his back, were covered with heavy tissue where there should have been skin. It was horrible, especially as it was now, all laid open in big gashes inflicted by the whip.

I was crouched by Mr. Littlejohn, but somebody pushed me back and I lost my balance. It was Priddy, and he knelt and used the handle of the whip to further open the ripped shirt.

"There, Jonah! Show these good people what you always keep hidden! Look there, folks! See those scars? Let me tell you how they got there, how this man—"

Mr. Littlejohn pushed up and drove his fist into Priddy's face. Priddy's lip split. "I'll kill you," Mr. Littlejohn declared in a horrible voice. "I'll kill you right here." And he fell in on him, flinging blood with every motion.

Men yelled, moved in, and pulled him away from Priddy. Mr. Littlejohn shrugged them off like flies and stood trembling. Blood dripped down his back. He pointed down into Priddy's uplifted face. "You're a dead man if ever I see you again," he said.

"Thief! Coward!" Priddy spat back. "Tell them about how brave you were back on that train in Pennsylvania when you—"

Mr. Littlejohn kicked Priddy in the head, knocking him cold. He strode off, out of the ring, and began walking up Boot Hill. No one tried to stop him.

I went after him. By now he was a vague moving shape at the top of the hill. I came to the crest and saw him standing uncertainly only a few yards away.

"Mr. Littlejohn—it's me, Penn. Are you—"

He teetered and fell forward—and vanished.

For a moment I was confused but then realized he had fallen into one of the empty graves. Fortunately it had been partially refilled, so he didn't fall more than three feet or so.

I came to the narrow graveside. Mr. Littlejohn's big form filled it so there was no room for me to climb down beside him and help him rise. I knelt beside the hole. He was facedown, and his feet had not fallen into the hole, so he lay with knees bent and toes hooked on the foot of the grave.

I dug in my pocket for a match. The light shone down onto his back and once again I saw the ugly burn scars that covered it. No wonder he didn't remove his shirt when he fought—and no wonder Priddy had chosen a cloth-ripping bullwhip as the instrument by which to humiliate his old partner.

"Mr. Littlejohn, can you hear me?"

He moaned and pushed himself up, then shifted around until he was sitting in the bottom of the hole. "Penn?" His voice was tight and stressed. "That you?"

"Yes. Let me help you out."

But he got out mostly by himself. He laughed a pain-wracked little laugh. "It appears I'm somewhat like that little girl in Eldridge—resurrected from the grave."

"The only person who ever came out of a Boot Hill grave alive, I'd bet," I responded. "You got to get to a doctor. If infection sets in on those lash cuts you might wind up dead after all."

"Lord, but it hurts. Like knife slashes. Seems I'm destined to be the world's most scarred man, Penn."

"How'd you get burned?" I asked. Since he had brought up the matter, I hoped he wouldn't mind the question.

"Happened on a railraod. Maybe someday I'll tell you about it."

Together we went over Boot Hill into Dodge. I took Mr. Littlejohn to the dugout, cleaned his wounds as best I could, and put him in Primo's bed.

"I'm going after Dr. McCarty," I said. "You stay here, rest. He'll see you're taken proper care of."

"Obliged." He closed his eyes, trembling in pain he tried hard to conceal.

I had trouble finding McCarty, who had been called out elsewhere, and thus it was almost an hour before I and the doctor arrived back at the dugout. I opened the door and hurriedly led him in.

"Mr. Littlejohn, the doctor's here. We're going to get you—" I cut off, having just walked into the back room as I spoke. The doctor came in after me.

"Gone?" he asked.

"Gone," I said, looking at the bloodied, empty bed.

CHAPTER THIRTEEN

I tried to tell myself that Mr. Littlejohn was not my concern, that if he wanted to go off on his own, bleeding and hurt, that was his business. A half hour of restless tossing, though, proved I didn't believe my own argument. I got up, wondering why I couldn't just let the situation alone, and dressed. It was now past midnight.

I feared for Mr. Littlejohn's safety, not only because of his wounds, but because Priddy was still out there somewhere.

I got as far as the dugout door before I stopped, thinking. Returning to where my things were stored, I pulled out the wooden case containing Pa's 1875 Remington. I loaded the pistol and put it under my belt, then put on my jacket so the tail would hide the pistol butt. That I was breaking the law of Dodge I well knew, but it seemed essential. I felt an inexplicable sense of danger and didn't feel safe going out unarmed tonight.

GET
4 FREE BOOKS!

You can have the best Westerns delivered to your door for less than what you'd pay in a bookstore or online. Sign up for one of our book clubs today, and we'll send you 4 FREE* BOOKS, worth $23.96, just for trying it out...**with no obligation to buy, ever!**

———————◆◆◆———————

Authors include classic writers such as
LOUIS L'AMOUR, MAX BRAND, ZANE GREY
and more; PLUS new authors such as
COTTON SMITH, TIM CHAMPLIN, JOHNNY D. BOGGS
and others.

———————◆◆◆———————

As a book club member you also receive the following special benefits:
- **30% OFF** all orders through our website & telecenter!
- **Exclusive access** to special discounts!
- **Convenient** home delivery and 10 days to return any books you don't want to keep.

There is no minimum number of books to buy, and you may cancel membership at any time. See back to sign up!

*Please include $2.00 for shipping and handling.

YES! ☐

Sign me up for the Leisure Western Book Club and send my FOUR FREE BOOKS! If I choose to stay in the club, I will pay only $14.00* each month, a savings of $9.96!

NAME: _____

ADDRESS: _____

_____

TELEPHONE: _____

E-MAIL: _____

☐ **I WANT TO PAY BY CREDIT CARD.**

☐ VISA ☐ MasterCard ☐ DISCOVER

ACCOUNT #: _____

EXPIRATION DATE: _____

SIGNATURE: _____

Send this card along with $2.00 shipping & handling to:

**Leisure Western Book Club
20 Academy Street
Norwalk, CT 06850-4032**

Or fax (must include credit card information!) to: 610.995.9274.
You can also sign up online at www.dorchesterpub.com.

*Plus $2.00 for shipping. Offer open to residents of the U.S. and Canada only.
Canadian residents please call 1.800.481.9191 for pricing information.
If under 18, a parent or guardian must sign. Terms, prices and conditions subject to change. Subscription subject
to acceptance. Dorchester Publishing reserves the right to reject any order or cancel any subscription.

It was cool outside. As far north of the dead line as I was, I could still hear music and voices from south of it. Dodge never slept during the cattle season; places like the Lady Gay ran full tilt around the clock.

I walked southward on Third Avenue and on down past the dead line to Locust, where I turned left. Music and noise poured out of the Varieties Dance Hall and the nearby Lady Gay. Walking on past them, I came to the Great Western, which loomed up impressively against the dark sky. It was an attractive building with a broad front porch and a railed balcony. I stepped up onto the porch and through the door.

The night clerk was dozing behind the desk and did not awaken. I walked quietly past and on up to Mr. Littlejohn's room. Its door was not fully closed, but I knocked softly. No answer. I pushed it open, fearing I would find him passed out or dead in there.

"Mr. Littlejohn?"

No one responded. I walked in, fumbled for matches, and lit a lamp.

The room was empty, but the bed was rumpled and had bloodstains on it. Mr. Littlejohn had come back here and lay down, at least briefly. Drawers hung open in a chest in the corner, and the wardrobe door was ajar. He had gathered his goods, as if to leave.

For which I couldn't blame him, given the abuse he had taken in the fight. But he was in no shape to travel.

I wondered, if in fact Mr. Littlejohn was leaving

Dodge, if he was going to take the medicine show wagon. Priddy might already have found and reclaimed it; the thing wasn't hard to spot, after all. I went to the window and looked out to see if it was still parked below.

Somewhat to my surprise, it was. And something else: a man, it appeared, beside the wagon, moving a little. Maybe Mr. Littlejohn was getting some of Dr. Demorest's Radical Purge to cut his pain. But a closer look at the shadowed figure revealed it was too small a man to be Mr. Littlejohn. Suddenly the man slumped heavily against the wagon and fell. He did not get up.

Cold prickles ran down my back. It might be just some drunk passing out down there. Or maybe it was someone hurt.

I had to check, though I dreaded doing so. I left the room, rushed down the stairs, and passed the still-sleeping night clerk. I eased the front door shut behind me and hurried around to the wagon.

The man still lay there. I went to his side and knelt. "Sir?"

He moaned. I struck a match and rather tremblingly held it aloft.

The light fell on the face of Winfred Priddy. I moved the match down his form and saw thick blood on his chest. He had been stabbed.

"Mr. Priddy? Can you hear me?"

His closed eyes half opened. His lips moved thickly. "Jonah . . . Jonah had a knife. . . ."

I felt sick to my stomach. "I'll get you help," I said. The match burned down to my fingers and I threw it aside. By the time I struck and held up a second one, I was looking down at the face of a corpse.

I stood and turned away, straining not to become ill. After a couple of minutes I got more control of myself and took several deep breaths.

What should I do? Alert Earp, Bassett, Masterson? Probably. Yet I couldn't. Perhaps it was fear or confusion—but the idea of bringing Priddy's death to the attention of the law repelled me.

I didn't know what to do about this—so I did nothing but head for the dugout at a dead run, feeling not much like a man right now; more like a kid facing something he couldn't handle.

Halfway back, I stopped, panting and dripping with sweat, at the intersection of Second Avenue and Front Street, and leaned against the city well, again fighting nausea. Finally I stumbled over to the outside staircase up the side of Wright, Beverley & Company, and put my head in my hands.

When I looked up again, the eastern sky was paling; sunrise was near. I was still seated on the steps, my left shoulder against the brick wall. Somebody was driving a wagon past and looking at me rather peculiarly. I had slept with my eyes open.

Rising, I plodded slowly back to Primo's dugout.

The knock came at midmorning, and I rose from my blankets to answer with heart already pounding. It was the law, no doubt. The only question was which officer it would be.

Masterson. That wasn't good; I would have to endure the intense gaze of those knowing eyes.

"Come in, Sheriff," I said, and he did.

He looked around. "You've neatened up the place considerable since you came here. Where's Primo?"

"Out bone hunting."

"Uh-huh." He swept his eyes around the room again. "Had a death in town last night, Penn."

"Oh. That's bad." My pulse raced.

"Indeed. They always are. A medicine show man from Kansas City, this one was. Fellow name of Winfred Priddy." He looked at me as he said the name, closely watching my reaction.

"I'm sorry to hear that," I said.

"I suppose you are. He was the former partner of your friend Jonah Littlejohn, you may know."

"Yes."

"It's my understanding they must have had a falling out—because Priddy showed up at a little fight staged northwest of town last night. It's also my understanding he put Mr. Littlejohn into a bad situation with a bullwhip. But you wouldn't know about that—you don't attend such fights as that, do you?"

"The fact is, I did attend that fight."

Masterson's eyes burned their cool fire into me. "Now that you mention it . . . I think someone did say you were there. And that you tried to intervene on Mr. Littlejohn's behalf."

"Yes."

"And that you went after him when he left."

"I did." I was doing my best not to tremble. The room felt terribly cold to me, though Masterson seemingly didn't notice it.

"And what happened after that, Penn?"

Masterson certainly had talked to Mr. McCarty; he wanted to see if I would tell the same story.

"I put Mr. Littlejohn into Primo's bed and went after Dr. McCarty. I had a bit of trouble finding him, and when we got back here, Mr. Littlejohn was gone."

Masterson picked thoughtfully at his mustache and nodded. "And you don't know where he went?"

"No sir."

"That's too bad. I'd surely like to talk to him right now."

I had to ask: "You suspect he killed Priddy?"

He smiled again. "What do you suspect?"

"I'm not an officer. I don't know much about this sort of thing."

"Let me ask you something straight out, Penn—are you covering for Jonah Littlejohn? Hiding him?"

"No sir," I said firmly. "I haven't seen him since I left him on that bed back there. I swear it."

Masterson nodded and tapped his cane on the floor. Once again he looked around the room. "Yes sir, you certainly have improved the looks of Primo's place."

He went back to the door. "Penn, can I find you here if I need you?"

"Most likely. Or at Dan Johnson's, if he has work for me."

"You see Jonah Littlejohn, you come straight to me or one of the other officers—hear?"

"Yes sir. Thank you, Mr. Masterson."

"Thank you, Penn. By the way, plan to stay in town for the time being, huh?"

My knees felt like rubber. I could say nothing.

Masterson walked out, whistling. His limp was a little more evident today. Maybe it was the morning air.

I closed the door and went back to bed, wondering what was going to come of all this and why I hadn't gone to Wichita instead of Dodge when I left Eldridge.

I didn't leave the dugout until late in the day. Lying in my blankets, I stared at the door until the afternoon was mostly gone, for some reason expecting it to open and reveal Mr. Littlejohn at any moment. It was a crazy expectation, for Mr. Littlejohn obviously had good reason to get as far away from Dodge as possible.

The door never opened and Mr. Littlejohn never appeared. Hours ticked past; the dugout was silent except for the scurrying of vermin in the corners—so silent that when a big orange centipede crawled up the wall beside me I could actually hear its motion.

In the afternoon I made my first meal of the day, but barely picked at it. All I could see in my mind was the bloody form of Winfred Priddy, stabbed and dead beside the medicine show wagon. I didn't want to eat.

As the day waned I finally went outside and walked toward the wagon shop. Dan Johnson was the kind of man whom it was comfortable to be around, and I needed such company just now. In the back of my mind I was toying with the notion of telling him everything and asking his advice on what I should do.

He was rimming a wheel when I walked in. He looked up at me, sweat beaded on his brow.

"Howdy, Penn. You look a bit the worse for the wear."

"Hard night last night."

He grinned. "I didn't take you for the carousing type."

"Not carousing. Just a hard night. Didn't sleep well."

He looked at me ponderingly, then seemed to become uncomfortable. "Penn, if it's money you're worrying over—"

"Not money. Nothing. It's nothing."

He obviously wasn't sure what to make of me at the moment and probably wondered why I had come. I was beginning to wonder the same thing, for I had already decided I couldn't yet bring myself to tell Dan what had happened.

He finished his work on the wheel, and I complimented the job. He went over to the stove, where a coffeepot sat, always hot, and poured two steaming cupfuls.

"Something wrong, Penn?" he asked as he gave me mine.

"No, really, it's nothing."

He took a sip. "You hear about the murder?"

"Yes." *Don't talk about that,* my mind yelled at him. *Don't bring it up at all.*

"They say he was stabbed real bad. All bloody. He was beside that medicine show wagon you fixed, you know."

"I heard."

"They think his old partner did it. He's a strong

man who was in a fight up beyond Boot Hill earlier in the night. They say the fellow who wound up dead came with a whip and beat the strong man until—"

I put down my cup abruptly. "I got to go, Dan. Thanks for the coffee." I felt him watching me as I left and knew he wondered why I was acting so strangely.

"Penn!" he called after me when I was half a block away. I stopped and turned; he waved me back.

"What is it?"

"I forgot to tell you. Somebody came by here looking for you this morning."

Masterson, I figured. "Who?"

"I didn't know them. There were three of them. Riders in long coats, and they asked for you by name." He paused. "I told them I didn't know you. There was something about them I didn't like. Do they sound familiar?"

"Yes," I said. "They do."

"Who are they?"

It seemed colder than ever now, even though, for some reason, I was sweating. "I wish I knew."

I sat in the dark corner of a saloon, having ordered beer in hopes it would calm my nerves. But so far I hadn't touched it. I marveled numbly over the ways the blessings and blows of life fall all together. Within a span of less than two days I had been handed more money than I had ever possessed before at one time and had gone through a strange but enticing encounter with the beautiful young Melanie Fain. But I had also seen Mr. Littlejohn humiliated and his mysterious scars exposed and had watched Winfred Priddy die, apparently killed by my own friend. Now, as if all that were not enough, I had discovered from Dan Johnson that the three unknown riders who had apparently sought me in Eldridge had somehow traced me to Dodge.

How they had done so had mystified me until mere moments ago, when I had picked up from an adjacent table a copy of the most recent edition of the Dodge City *Times* and by chance had noticed a story on the back page. I had read it four times now, maybe in the hope that the words would somehow change and this yet-one-more unwelcome truth— the most unwelcome yet—would simply dissolve like the bubbles in the warm and untouched beer before me. But each time I read it, it was the same, black words couched in the colorful Times language:

The town of Eldridge, recently famed as the place where the dead rise again, has been visited by the reaper once more in a fashion expected to be of the more permanent variety.

Killed by brutal knifing were an elderly man and wife named Halley, and another elder Eldridgian, a merchant named Ramm.

The Halley couple were found in their home, the old man's body pitifully across that of the woman as if he had vainly tried to shield her from the murderer's grim blade. Halley was known as a capable wagon maker and a respected member of his community.

The merchant Ramm, also widely known and liked, died in his own home, apparently at the hands of the same ruffian or ruffians who killed the married pair. No one in the grief-stricken town has ventured a guess at any reason for the murders.

It is told to this correspondent, though, that speculation is rampant concerning a young man, recently disappeared from custody of the Halleys, who is thought by some to be an as-yet-unfound fourth victim of the murderer, or perhaps to be the murderer himself. His name is, or perhaps was, Pennington Malone.

Young Malone was born of criminal heritage, it is said, and was reported to have disliked the Halleys who raised him, though he was equally said to be a close friend of the murdered merchant Ramm.

The peace officers of Dodge have been notified by wire to keep their eyes open.

I wasn't prone to cry much; I had gone through loss and abuse for years without shedding a tear. But now it was difficult for me to choke back the tears from my eyes, for the world had turned black and hellish all around me. Right now I could even have wept for the Halleys, harsh as they had been to me. But my real grief was for poor Mr. Ramm, for I figured he must have suffered before he died— suffered so much that he obviously had broken down and told his assailants that Penn Malone had left him a note saying he was gone to Dodge. And then they had knifed him until he was dead. Probably the Halleys had suffered similarly; I suppose that under torture Old Halley must have told the killers Mr. Ramm was my friend and that maybe he might know where I had gone.

Whatever had happened, I was obviously being hunted, and hunted seriously, by three brutal men I didn't know, and for reasons of which I had no clue.

And now they were in Dodge.

CHAPTER FOURTEEN

To leave Dodge at once seemed the only sensible option, but I could not do that. First I would need my pistol and supplies back at the dugout. To travel speedily would require a horse—and that I would have to buy. At least I had remaining most of the money Fain had paid me.

I tore the story from the newspaper and put it into my pocket. After paying for my untouched beer I left the saloon. The sun had set and it was dark outside. Good. In the night I could hide.

I walked the darkest routes back to the dugout, looking around every corner, inspecting every window below which I must pass. Dodge no longer seemed the exciting, free place it initially had. Now it seemed a dangerous maze.

I heard horse hooves on the street and flattened against a wall. Two men rode by, neither looking at me. They were unfamiliar. I was about to move on when I heard boots on a boardwalk and saw Wyatt

Earp walk past, only a few yards away. He sauntered along, looking about, and I thought he had seen me. But apparently he hadn't, for he walked on by.

It put me in mind that I was not only in danger of the three riders pursuing me, but also of the law. The newspaper story had said the Dodge peace officers had been notified to keep an eye out for Penn Malone, former ward of an Eldridge wagon maker. How long would it take them to surmise that the young newcomer Penn Corey, who worked at a wagon shop and had come from Eldridge, was really Penn Malone? Surely they had figured it out already. Masterson was not the sort past whom such a thing would slip. Perhaps Earp really had been trying to follow me when he passed.

I took a roundabout path and got to the dugout slowly. For a moment or two, standing at the door, I considered going to the law and turning myself in for my own safety. I was, after all, not guilty of killing anyone, whatever other people thought, and I knew who the real killers were, or at least probably were. Yet I really didn't. Three riders . . . how much information was that for a law officer to go on? If I showed up at the door of Masterson or Bassett with no more to say for myself than that, I would have little hope of being believed.

The dugout was dark, but I was wary of striking a light. Perhaps the riders had learned where I was living and were watching the place, waiting for my return. But if so, surely they had already seen me. With that thought I went ahead and lit the lamp on the table.

Yellow light spilled out across the room. I watched

a mouse dart away toward a hole in the corner. What a dark, dank place this was—like living in a cave. A far cry from Nigel Fain's fine house.

Fain. I suddenly remembered the offer he had made—if I needed help, come to him. Well, I needed something now: safety. Sanctuary.

Hope soared. I had an option besides flight. If I could only make it to Fain's house across town, surely there I would be safe. I could ask Fain for protection and secrecy, time to think things through and deal with the situation. If that was a house of secrets, as the Locust Man had said, then I could become one of them.

I gathered my clothing and stuffed it into the bag. My pistol I put into my belt, under my jacket. I wished I could wear the gunbelt itself, openly flaunt the weapon so that all could see I was not to be bothered. But not in Dodge, especially not when I did not want the eye of the law on me.

When you live in a dugout awhile, Primo had said, you develop an ear for certain sounds. My dugout residency had been brief so far, but my ear must already have been honed a bit, for I heard the snake slither even before it sounded its rattle. I froze in place, then picked it out—coiled in a corner, rattle fluttering, head moving and weaving as the tongue flicked at me.

I slowly picked up a cast-iron kettle from beside the stove and, advancing with it before me, put it down quickly over the rattler before it could strike. Grabbing a broom, I lifted the edge of the kettle a little, stuck the broom beneath, and worked the snake into the kettle, which I uprighted and lidded very quickly. The snake rattled and slithered inside for a few moments, then became silent. I wasn't sure how I would get rid of the thing, but at least it was safely confined.

I finished my work and slipped on my hat, and then the front door burst open.

A tall man stood there. His face was dark and ugly, and I recognized it as the face of one of the men who had pursued me that night in Eldridge.

He grinned. "Hello there, Penn Malone. You're the spitting image of your daddy, you are." He drew a Colt revolver from his gunbelt, leveled it on me. "You'll be coming with me now."

Inspiration, Pa had always said, is an angel that descends to help you when you need it, and never a moment before. I needed it now, and it did not fail me.

"Please . . ." I said, dropping my bag, backing off with hands upraised. "Please, I'm not well, I . . ." And I fell to the floor and feined unconsciousness. I let my hand drop to the lid of the kettle that held the rattler.

The man frowned and holstered his pistol. "Hey, what's wrong with you! Get up!" He came toward me.

All in a motion I grabbed the kettle, flung off the lid, and heaved the contents at the man. The snake writhed in the air. The man screamed, and then it was on him and sank fangs into his left arm. He tore the snake loose, flung it against the wall, and pulled his pistol. Still screaming, he fired three quick shots that tore up the fat snake—and then he turned the pistol on me.

I already had mine out, and fired. It was the first

time I had ever shot at a man, and maybe that's why I missed. As I was about to get off a second shot, another man raced through the front door and knocked down the gun arm of the snakebit man. A bullet that would have shattered my skull passed harmlessly into the floor. The arrival of the second man kept me from firing an immediate second shot, for I didn't know if he was one of the three riders or perhaps some passerby responding to the gunfire, trying to help me.

"Don't kill him, Spano!" the second man said. "And for damn sure don't shoot anymore! You want to draw the law?"

That answered my question about his motivation. I releveled my pistol. "I don't know who you are, but I'm getting out of here right now," I said. "Out of my way."

"He threw a rattler on me!" the man called Spano said. Spano . . . where had I heard that name? "It bit me, bit me right on the arm!"

"Out of my way," I ordered again.

The second man swore and drew his pistol incredibly fast. His shot hammered into the flesh of my shoulder, numbing me to the ends of my fingers. My pistol dropped; blood ran down my arm.

"I didn't want to have to make more racket, but you didn't give me any choice," he said. "Now let's move, before the law gets here."

"I'm going to die," Spano said. He began crying. "It's swelling already, Potter." Potter . . . another name that touched my memory.

I was moving my fingers to make sure I still could. My arm still felt numb, but now dull pain was spreading through my shoulder. I looked at the bleeding wound, noting thankfully that it was no more than a deep crease. I felt sure this Potter, who had such obvious skill on the draw, had deliberately shot me in such a way as to minimize the damage. And he had told the other not to kill me—which made me think that, whatever they wanted me for, I was precious merchandise.

Spano, crying harder now, said, "Whitey . . . where's Whitey? He'll know what to do. I don't want to die, Potter. I want a doctor."

Potter ignored him. He came to me, grabbed me by my good shoulder, and shoved me toward the door. I resisted, and he drew his pistol and struck me in the head, hard. Everything spun, became fluid, deep, warm, and I sank into it. Just before it covered me I realized who these men were.

I never knew how they got me out of Dodge, nor how they evaded the law, given the number of shots that had been fired. Someone surely had come to investigate the gunfire, but must have gotten there too late, for when I came to I was still a prisoner. They must have had horses waiting near the dugout and ridden away fast—and from the way my midsection felt, I seemingly had done my riding draped belly-down over somebody's saddlehorn.

I was inside a sod building, this one built of blocks of sod, rather than dug into a hillside like Primo's. A coal oil lantern burned on a table in the center of the room. I was lying on a rough pile of sacks and ragged, stinking blankets. A man with a very thick shock of white hair was cleaning a pistol in the corner—not just any pistol, either, but mine. Potter was rolling a cigarette and looking out the door of the sod house, and across the room from me, on a tick mattress lying on the dirt floor, Spano was writhing, his left arm as big around as his head. There were saddles in the corner.

Potter finished rolling his cigarette, cranked up the wick and lit the tobacco at the top of the chimney, then cranked the wick down again.

He got up, went over to Spano, and stood there looking down at him and smoking. Spano was suffering terribly.

"Spano, I think you're going to die," Potter said flatly.

Spano moaned and flailed some more. Potter drew on his cigarette and walked over to the white-haired man. They talked quietly; I caught only a little of what they said, but enough to tell they were debating about what to do with Spano.

Spano . . . Spano . . . Pete Spano. That was his name. I remembered it now. Pa had talked a lot about his new companion Spano back when he was starting to get on the edge of the law. And Potter, too—Potter Griggs. But the white-haired man, who must be the Whitey that Spano had mentioned, was new to me.

I was a prisoner of two former associates of my father, and a third man. But why? What did they plan for me—and why had Potter been so eager to keep me alive?

Potter walked back across the room to Spano. He bent over and talked directly into Spano's face, like people do sometimes with bedridden old folks who can hardly hear.

"We'll try to get you some help," Potter said. "But not until Moreland arrives."

"I'm sick, Potter. Hurting."

"I know. I know. We'll have you in good shape soon. You hang on until Moreland gets here."

Moreland . . . a name I didn't know. I lay still, listening. So far they had not detected I had come to, and I wanted to keep it that way for now. Perhaps I could ascertain what all this was about.

I took an inventory of my situation, analyzing the dull throb in my shoulder, the ache in my middle, the pain in my skull. I was banged up, but did not think my injuries serious. I could tell more certainly if I tried to move, but that would draw my captors' attention.

Interestingly, I wasn't as afraid anymore. Some reserve of calm and strength nourished me, and my mind was clear. Even though I did not know why I was held or what was planned for me, I felt confident that some escape could be made. After all, through my own resourcefulness I had inflicted a likely fatal injury on one of them. If I could manage that, what else might I be able to do?

Whitey had finished cleaning Pa's Remington and held it up to examine it. "Pretty gun," he said. "Worth Malone does have an eye for weaponry." Worth Malone—my father. Did all of this have to do with him? I couldn't see how, with him back in Leavenworth.

Thunder rumbled outside, once very lowly, then loudly. Potter went back to the door.

"Moreland's going to get wet," he observed. He paced about for a moment, then looked back at me.

I closed my eyes as he came back toward me. I felt him lean over me. More thunder, then the sound of rain, sudden and heavy.

Potter lightly slapped my cheek, and I blinked involuntarily. No point in pretending now. I opened my eyes.

"Why, howdy, boy," Potter said. "Wake up and say hello to a soon-to-be-rich man."

Potter talked to me for the next ten minutes as rain gushed from the sky and dripped at myriad places through the sod house's dirt roof. Talked, yet told me nothing that really explained why they had taken me.

And one thing he said made no sense to me at all—that Pa was free, and that the man named Moreland had been out for weeks trying to locate him. I shook my head.

"My Pa's in Leavenworth," I said. "He would have written me if he had gotten out . . . would have come for me."

Potter shook his head as he rolled another cigarette. He had smoked one after another. "No, boy. Worth Malone walked out of that prison a free man a full year ago. I watched him do it. Why do you think he'd have told you? I shared his cell, so I know for a fact he hadn't answered any letter of yours for a long, long time. He was ashamed to, boy. Ashamed to be no more than a sorry prisoner with nothing to give his own son."

"I don't believe he would have got out without telling me," I said stubbornly. But inside I did believe it; Pa had, after all, let all contact with me drop.

I had been convinced for a long time he didn't care anything about me. But I would never admit that to Potter. Anyway, in one way of looking at it, what Potter said indicated Pa did care a bit about me, if only enough to be ashamed of himself where I was concerned. That was at least a spark of fatherly caring, even if not a full flame.

Over in the far corner Whitey cussed and moved; a stream of rainwater had started falling directly on his head. A good six or seven such streams poured out here and there around the ceiling, wetting the dirt floor to mud. One was pouring directly onto Spano, adding to his torment. He groaned and writhed some more, but his two partners still ignored him.

"What are you going to do with me?" I asked.

"Why, nothing more than reunite you with your father—if he does what we want. If he doesn't, we'll just have to take it from there. And that's about all you need to know, boy."

"What do you want with my father?"

"You know more than you need to already."

Spano groaned terribly, twisting like the rattler that had bitten him. The rain gushed down outside, and now a second leak opened above Spano, and he now seemed so pitiful I almost wished I had not thrown the rattler at him, even though I know he would not have hesitated to have done far worse to me.

CHAPTER FIFTEEN

Potter brought over some rope and tied my hands together, then ran the rope down and bound my ankles. "Can't have you trying something foolish now that you're awake," he said.

I kept my wrists tensed and bulged as he tied them, hoping that when I relaxed the rope might be loose enough to slip. But he pulled it tight despite that.

At least my part of the roof wasn't leaking. Poor Spano was being drenched and nobody seemed to care. Obviously they had written him off; it seemed to me that if they planned to do nothing for him, it would almost be a kindness to take him out and shoot him. His arm was gruesome, swollen like an overripe plum and discolored.

Potter seemed restless and repeatedly said he wished Moreland would get back. Whitey, who so far had ignored me completely and seemed calm as a lazy hound, said the rain probably slowed up Moreland, and especially the lightning, because

Moreland was afraid of lightning. Which showed that Moreland, whatever else he was, was no fool; lightning in these parts was a real threat. A man in Eldridge had been hit by a bolt while he was carrying two milk buckets. The buckets melted in what was left of his hands.

The sun was just beginning to come up now; the rain-driven plains outside the door were turning a dismal light gray. I was glad to see the morning, for it had been one unpleasant night, to say the least.

Rain gushed, never slackening. The streams pouring in on Spano were bigger than before; had he been lying a little differently, he might have drowned in one of them. He had stopped moaning now except a couple of times a minute.

Potter and Whitey dug bread and jerky out of some saddlebags in the corner and ate. My own stomach was empty as a cavern, but I had too much pride to ask food of them. I lay there and watched them eat. Meanwhile, I heard an unusual, deep noise like some great weight shifting, settling. Where it came from or what it was I couldn't tell.

Potter had been squatting on the floor, but suddenly he leaped to his feet and pointed out the door. "Yonder he comes!" he exclaimed. The laconic Whitey merely grunted and nodded.

A few minutes later a drenched man came through the door, carrying his saddle, wearing a dripping slicker and a beaver hat with the brim soaked so that it sagged down around his ears. He had a heavy but short wiry brown beard and a long nose that was thick between eyes that seemed to jump out at you like bullets. He looked straight at me as he entered and dumped his saddle by the others.

"I see you got the boy. Good."

Whitey held out a strip of jerky to the newcomer. "How'd you fare, Moreland?" Whitey sounded very southern. Georgia, maybe South Carolina.

"Good and bad. Good part is I found him. Bad part is, he looks to be sick, and he's got somebody with him."

"Who?"

"Don't know."

"Where are they?"

"Southeast of Dodge a ways."

Potter pursed his lips. "Having somebody with him could complicate things."

"It already has. I could have dealt with him myself if it hadn't been for that other one. But remember, there's four of us and just two of them."

"Three of us, you mean," Whitey said. "Have you noticed Spano back yonder?"

"Yeah. What's wrong with him?"

"Snakebit."

"What?"

"The boy yonder threw a rattler on Spano when he went in to get him."

Moreland took that in for a second, then threw back his head and laughed heartily. "Now, if that don't beat it! Throwed a rattler on Spano!"

Spano moaned. His voice was very soft; it was like he was a long way from here. I didn't see how he could survive much longer, but knew he might. Snakebite victims sometimes take hours to die.

Moreland looked about the place. "You surely did

pick you a leaky place for us to squat," he commented. He came back to look me over.

I stared him in the eye as he inspected me. Would have spit in it except I had never been an accurate spitter beyond three feet or so. "Hello there, boy," he said. "I seen your pa not long ago."

So that *had* been Pa he was talking about. I had wondered. The part about him being sick worried me.

"Your pa's looking for you, you know it? Got something he wants to give you. Something that belongs to me."

Still staring him in the eye, I said, "I need to go outside."

"Why's that?"

"I been lying here listening to all this water dripping down. Makes you want to make some of your own, you know."

He laughed. I heard the same low, sagging, shifting sound as before; nobody else seemed to notice it, but it concerned me. I didn't show it, though. Just kept staring Moreland in the eye.

"I think I'm going to like you, boy. Sure. You step out and do what you need, but if you run I'll be on you like fire on a match."

They didn't untie me, so I had to hop to the door. The clouds were so thick that the morning seemed sluggish, feeble, more like late evening; you couldn't really call what filtered through the clouds full-fledged light.

I walked out into the rain and fumbled with my trouser buttons. All the while I looked around, hoping to spot something to indicate where I was. But I saw no landmark. The land here was slightly rolling.

"Get back in here, boy!" Potter hollered out at me after a bit.

"Just a minute! This isn't easy with tied hands, you know." I was deliberately being slow.

I suddenly caught my breath. Something in the distance, just coming out from behind a long, low undulation of the landscape. My heart raced; wild hope surged.

It was a wagon, long and low and familiar, piled with bones. It was a long way off, but I could see it, moving along through the rain.

The yell burst from within me: "Primo! Primo! Help me—I'm here! Primo!"

And then somebody grabbed me roughly from behind and pulled me down. I struggled, hearing Potter curse. His fist struck me and made my ears ring. As he dragged me back through the mud toward the dugout, I twisted my head around and sank into despair, for the bone wagon had not stopped. It rolled along steadily through the rain, heading east.

Back inside, I knew it probably was just as well. Primo could have done nothing anyway, except get himself killed. Yet seeing him so close in this time of danger, then watching him drive away, was profoundly depressing. I sank back into my bed of rags and stared at the underside of the roof, which now looked like two slanting walls of mud, relatively dry above me, but dripping and oozing elsewhere.

Whitey leaned over me. "One more trick like that,

one more, and I'll gutshoot you and tack you to the wall to die."

"I don't think so," I said. "I don't know what you need me for, but I know you need me alive."

He pulled back his fist and hit me in the jaw; pain radiated through my skull. I closed my eyes and refused to react.

"If that wagon comes around again, I'll drop the driver off the seat. You don't want to be responsible for an innocent man's death, now, do you?"

"Innocent—like an old couple and an old widower storekeeper in Eldridge?"

He grinned slowly. "You were right hard to find, boy. We had no choice but to go inquiring. That storekeeper, he never did tell where you were. Spano found a note."

Good, courageous Mr. Ramm, I thought. So he had gone to his death without betraying me after all. Hot tears threatened to boil out of my eyes, but I squelched them, unwilling to show any emotion to these cold men.

Spano now was very near death. He moved only a little and moaned deep in his throat. Potter was pacing about at the front of the dugout; since my attempt to communicate with Primo, he had been raging furiously. It was obvious that, whatever these men planned, I was a vital part of it, and Pa was, too.

Apparently Moreland's job had been locating Pa, while the task of the other three had been finding and kidnapping me. Pa must have something they wanted quite badly, and I must be the pawn they would use to get it. But what could Pa possibly have? He had always been poor as a beggar, even before his time in prison. And I had never thought of prison as being a likely place to make money.

Moreland was standing by Spano's bed now, examining the dying man closely. "Whitey, think we ought to just shoot him?" he asked.

Whitey leaned over and looked into Spano's bleary, red-rimmed eyes. He went up toward the front of the dugout, Moreland with him, and talked it over with Potter. Rain still fell in torrents outside. Through the door I saw a jagged bolt of lightning crackle through the sky.

"Seems the only Christian thing to do," Potter said. "The old boy's about gone anyway."

Moreland drew his pistol and they started back toward Spano. I started to turn my head to the wall, not wanting to see the shot, and thus almost missed seeing the soaked, heavy roof of the dugout suddenly cave in—a huge mass of mud, rock, and wood that fell full weight on Spano, mashing him like a bug beneath a boot. Moreland, Potter, and Whitey all were suddenly cut off from me, buried under the front section of the roof. Only the portion of the roof above me, the driest portion, stayed up at all, so I avoided Spano's terrible fate. Still, heavy mud splattered down on me, and when I looked around I was trapped in a dark enclosure, a tiny sealed chamber inside a mass of sodden earth.

So that's what that deep, unidentifiable noise had been—an old sod house roof about to fall in, as such sometimes did in heavy rains.

I pushed up on my elbows. My oozing prison was narrow, and it would be only a matter of minutes before the remaining roof fell on me like it had on the others. Were they all dead? Spano was, certainly. I listened, trying to pick out voices, and thought I heard a groan, though it could merely have been more sounds from the resettling mud.

It was dark in here, but not fully dark. Pinpoint light came in through the roof, little holes created when the mass shifted and fell. I wanted to claw at the holes, but my ropes kept me from it. Beside me a little more of the roof gave way and fell. It almost hit me, but also helped pull open the hole above me, making it into a large crack.

Blast these ropes! While I was tied I could not possibly enlarge that hole and climb out. But I had no knife, nothing to get through the rope. Once again that deep noise of shifting weight came. In moments I would be buried like the others.

A shadow passed over the opening above, and my spirit alternately soared, then sank. If someone were there, he could help me out—but who would it be except one of my captors? Perhaps one or all of the survivors had struggled free.

Still, I could not survive remaining here, so I raised a yell. Immediately burly hands began clawing wildly at the crack, pulling it wider and knocking mud down into my face. Rain swept in through the opening, then an arm came down. There was a face above, looking in, but I could not clearly see it.

"Take my arm, Penn," Primo Smith said.

I almost shouted in joy. He had heard my earlier yell after all. "I can't reach you, Primo. I'm tied."

At that he withdrew his arm, then put it back through again with a knife in hand. He dropped it and I managed to pick it up and begin cutting at my bonds.

Meanwhile, Primo began digging more, ripping away big clots of wet dirt. Now he was more visible. Soaked to the skin, he labored furiously, his hat sending off sheets of water from its brim. Suddenly a big chunk of roof fell off from the place he was working, almost pitching him in and dumping its heavy weight atop me. I fell back.

"You all right, Penn?" Primo called in.

"Yeah," I said. "Yeah. Just knocked me down." I had lost his knife and had to dig around for it. When I found it I quickly finished cutting through my ropes and pulled my hands and feet free.

I gave him back his knife handle-first, then he reached in to me. His broad, powerful hands closed about my wrists and pulled me up. I put my feet against the wall and shimmied out into the open. It was marvelous to be free; even the driving rain was a pleasure.

I looked around. No sign of my captors.

"There's others buried in there, Primo," I said. "They may be alive." Indeed, I could imagine I again heard movement, and a muffled voice, through the noise of the rain. But I couldn't be sure.

"How many?"

"Maybe three alive. The fourth is dead for sure."

"Who are they?"

"Kidnappers. Killers."

"Leave them, then," he said. "We ain't in no position to haul in three bad men."

"Leave them?" The idea seemed callous. Then I thought about what they had done to the Halleys and Mr. Ramm, and my pity drained away. Maybe there was some justice at work in this world after all.

The bone wagon sat off behind us some distance away. Primo had circled around to the rear after hearing my yell earlier.

"You're going to have to do some explaining to me," he said as he headed back toward the wagon. "But save it. Right now let's get to Dodge. We'll fire up the old dugout stove and make coffee and you can tell me all about what's going on here."

"Not the dugout," I said. "I can't go there. I want you to take me to Nigel Fain's, and when we get close to Dodge, I'll need to hide in the bones."

Primo looked at me like I had gone loco. "Penn, maybe you better start giving that explanation right now."

We rumbled southeast toward Dodge. The rain slackened to a drizzle. Primo listened silently to my story, reacting sometimes with nods and grunts, and when I was finished I asked if he believed me and if he would help me.

"Of course I believe you, and of course I'll help you. You helped me when I was cut, and I wasn't raised to forget those what aid me. Whether you're Penn Corey or Penn Malone makes no difference—you're the one who helped old Primo when he needed it, and now I'll help you however I can."

"Even though there are those who think I killed the Halleys and Mr. Ramm? Even though the only person who can prove that wrong appears to be a killer himself and likely wouldn't be believed?"

"I'll keep my mouth shut."

"Even if an old friend like Masterson asks you pointblank about me? Which he likely will."

Primo looked at me like he couldn't understand my persistence. "Penn, if you were the killing type, things might be different. But you ain't, and I got no problem with protecting the innocent. But there is something you need to think about, and that's that Fain may not let you hide at his place, not if you're being talked up as a likely murderer. Have you thought about that?"

"It's crossed my mind. But I figure it's a chance I have to take. To clear my name may take some resources I don't have, Primo. A man like Nigel Fain could make the difference for me, if he will. Besides, I think his daughter looks favorably at me, if you know what I mean. That can't hurt. And he did make me a promise."

Primo asked, "Where did they say your father is?"

"Somewhere southeast of Dodge."

Primo fell silent, like he was pondering something. At last he said, "Tell you what, Penn. If Fain gives you a place to hide, I'll take out to the southeast and see if I can find your pa. It'll be needle in a haystack, but who knows? Maybe I'll spot him. He alone?"

"They said there was a man with him. I don't know who. Thanks, Primo. I don't know what to say to you. I really do appreciate you."

He said, "Penn, don't start gushing like a dang female."

The bone wagon creaked on toward Dodge. The rain had finally stopped.

CHAPTER SIXTEEN

I rode into Dodge hidden beneath buffalo bones. We came in after dark so we could approach the Fain house without drawing much notice. I waited, uncomfortable among the limey bones, as Primo went to the door and gained entrance. When he came out again the Chinaman was with him, bearing a dark blanket that they threw across me as they hustled me into the house. Before I knew it, Primo was gone, I was closed away in an upstairs room, and the Chinaman was treating the bullet crease in my shoulder, which had become scabbed and ugly from lack of cleaning. But it hadn't hurt too badly until now, as he probed and dabbed at it.

"Will Mr. Fain be talking to me?" I asked.

"When ready, when ready," the Chinaman said. "Mr. Fain do anything only when ready."

"I hope he will. I need to talk to him."

"When ready."

I opened my mouth to ask about Melanie, but
didn't. The question would be wrongly taken.

The Chinaman, who told me his name was Hop
Lin, left me and half an hour later returned with a
meal on a tray. Stew, bread, coffee, pie—it was deli-
cious, and much appreciated by me. When I was
done, I selected a book at random from a loaded
case and lay down on the bed in the small but nicely
furnished room—I had expected nothing less in
Fain's house. Ironically, it was a volume of tales
about Robin Hood, and my eye went immediately to
the story of the hero's first meeting with Little John.
Of course that set me to thinking over unpleasant
recent memories, and I quickly put the book down.
My ordeal had exhausted me, anyway. I went to
sleep for the night.

Awakening me in late morning was Hop Lin with
breakfast. Later he came dragging in a big tin tub
and pail after pail of steaming water, a thick bar of
soap, and a pile of warm towels. He smiled, bowed,
and left me alone to enjoy the best bath of my life. I
lay back in the tub, letting the warm water soothe
me, as thin mists of steam rose toward the ceiling.
Sleep almost overtook me again.

As I relaxed there, half dozing, I wondered what
had become of Mr. Littlejohn. Thinking of him was
painful now, for now I thought of him as a killer.
Frankly, I also resented him a bit simply because my
association with him in the eyes of the local law
could only make me look worse.

When the tub grew cooler I climbed out, dried
and dressed, and began pacing about the room. I
had nothing to do, nowhere to go, and was not sure

what my standing here was. Was I to remain only in my room, or could I leave? I went to the door and opened it. The hall had no access to outside light and thus was rather dark. Looking down it, I saw a quick, familiar movement, the flash of an unforgettable dark eye, the closing of a door.

Melanie was there, down the hall in her own room.

Stepping out in the hall, I went toward her door, wanting to see her, talk to her. I passed the door to the room adjacent to mine; I heard something on the other side—maybe the scraping of a chair on the floor—then the voice of a woman and that of a man. The door opened and Hop Lin stepped out.

Beyond him, for a half second, I caught a glimpse of someone else, a woman in a long white gown. The face . . . I glimpsed it only for an instant and could not describe what I saw—but it left me with the impression of something distorted, twisted, even mutilated. My spine turned to ice.

Hop Lin seemed shocked to see me, and his thin face darkened in anger.

"You not to be here—you should be back in your room. Mr. Fain want you to stay until the time when he will see you."

"I'm sorry. I just thought that—"

"Back! Back in your room or he will be angry! Then you be thrown out and the law will come."

Hearing him talk so to me angered me a little, but there was nothing I could do. I turned and went back to my room.

Melanie, now I see how so fine a house can seem a prison, I thought, and wondered if I had been wise to seek Fain's sanctuary after all.

On the other side of my wall I heard a voice, feminine, muffled, and indistinct, and felt the same coldness in my spine. What had I seen? Who? Could that glimpsed figure be Melanie's mother? If so, what was wrong with her?

The Locust Man was right after all. This was a house of mysteries.

Nigel Fain came to the room well after dark. A single lamp burned on my bedside table. He was not in his wheelchair, but standing with crutches and a complicated-looking pair of leg braces that encased his pencil-thin, weak legs.

"I am told you were in the hall today," he said to me. His voice was cool.

"Yes," I responded. "I didn't know I was not supposed to be."

"When you are here, you must remain in this room. There are things here that are of no concern to those outside my family. They are not for outside eyes to see."

"Yes sir. I'm sorry."

His lips pursed into a very tight, formal smile. "There is no harm done, though. If you have seen anything you do not understand, merely put it out of your mind. And off your lips."

I nodded, taking it as a reference to the woman in the next room.

"Well, Mr. Malone—for I understand that is your true name—you are a young man most closely sought at the moment," Fain said. His tone was a little different, more formal. "They say you are sus-

pected of killing three people in the town of Eldridge from which you came."

"It isn't true," I said. "I didn't even know of the
deaths until I read about them in the newspaper
here. I realize there is nothing I can say to you to
prove my innocence, but I hope you can believe it."

"Is there no one who can testify you were elsewhere at the time they happened?"

That question I was almost afraid to answer, for I
remembered Mr. Littlejohn's unexplainable reaction
to the mere mention of Nigel Fain. What if Fain reacted similarly to mention of Mr. Littlejohn, as his
daughter had? Yet it seemed likely that Mr. Littlejohn's name, too, had made the local papers since
Priddy's killing.

In any case, I decided to answer vaguely. "There is
one man who could testify, but he is gone. I don't
know where to find him."

Fain put forward a crutch and swung one of his
dead legs forward. His face became tight with the
effort; it was the face of a degenerating man experienced in trying to mask pain. His braces made a
metallic squeak as he came close to my bedside.

His voice now was much softer; he almost whispered. "Is the man's name Jonah Littlejohn?"

I nodded.

A different kind of pain evidenced itself in his
face now. "So it is true," he said. "I had hoped all the
talk of these past days, the mention in the papers,
somehow was an error."

For a while, Mr. Fain was as good as gone from
me. He stared into the corner, and I wondered

what he was thinking. After a few moments he snapped back.

"And what is your relation to Mr. Littlejohn?" he asked, still keeping his voice low.

"Winfred Priddy, the man recently killed here, and Mr. Littlejohn were in—"

"Hush! Quieter! She will hear you!" he said sharply, cutting me off like a knife. Now I truly was confused. Obviously Mr. Littlejohn's name was a significant one around this house and one the woman in the next room was not supposed to hear.

Fain looked like he had said something he didn't intend to. "I am sorry," he said. "Disregard the comment—but do keep your voice very low."

"Yes sir. I was only saying that I saw Priddy and Mr. Littlejohn in a medicine show in Eldridge. They worked together. When I left Eldridge, I had stowed away in his wagon, more or less by accident. That was what threw us together. We had a falling out along the way after he got drunk, and I got off on my own again. Then I hitched another ride, this one with Primo Smith, the man who brought me here yesterday in the bone wagon. And that, beyond a time or two of us talking together here in Dodge, and me trying to help him when he got hurt in a fight, is the extent of my relationship with Mr. Littlejohn." I stopped, then risked a somewhat probing comment. "I gather, though, that yours is a little deeper."

"Indeed it is. And one that I had hoped was long past."

A long silence followed. Fain seemed to drift

away again. I could hear a cricket on the outside sill of my window.

Now seemed as good a time as any to lay my requests before him. "Mr. Fain," I said. "There's a lot here I don't understand, and since it isn't my business, I won't ask for explanation. All I want to tell you is that I am innocent of any crimes, and I know almost nothing about Jonah Littlejohn and absolutely nothing about whatever history you and he have together. Whatever that history is, I hope it will not cause you to look badly on me and decide not to help me after all, because God knows I do need help right now. Did Primo tell you what happened out on the prairie, about the men who captured me?"

Fain nodded.

"One of them said my father is somewhere southeast of here, sick. Primo has gone to try to find him, but I don't know if he will. And me, I'm trapped in a situation I don't know how to get out of. I'm accused of things I didn't do, I've been captured and threatened for reasons I don't understand, and now I'm caught in the middle of some old feud or problem between you and a man I became associated with sheerly by chance. Mr. Fain, you are a man of power and influence, I have to throw myself at your mercy and charity right now. I need advice, guidance, help of any sort you can give. I may have a long battle ahead to prove I am not a killer."

He had listened closely, and he nodded. "Yes. It could be long and difficult for you. That I know." He turned, making his braces squeak again, and looked out the window. "I know much about long and difficult battles, young Malone. I have fought many of them. Against business enemies, political enemies . . . against the steady decline of my own body. Some battles are neatly won or lost. Others seem to be decided slowly, or never at all." He shifted again in his braces. "I believe you are innocent. I have learned to read people in my years in business, and I read you as one falsely accused. And in any case, when you helped my daughter, I made to you a pledge of my availability should you need me. If that seemed a big pledge to you, remember that I am a man who does big things. That simply is my way, just as it is my way to keep my word. Any help you need, you will have."

"Thank you, sir." It was honestly difficult to hold back tears at that moment.

Fain said, "Now, what is it you wish me to do?"

Faced so directly with that question, I realized I had no clear answer. I told him as much, and he smiled, this time in an almost fatherly way.

"When we face unusual difficulties, our options do not always seem clear at once. Perhaps I may suggest one: Allow me to send for one of my attorneys. He is in Wichita and it will take some time for him to arrive, but he will be of tremendous help to you. If anyone can chart a course out of these waters, he can. In fact, young friend, I may need some navigation myself, for here I am harboring a wanted fugitive in my own home."

I had not thought of it that way before; it made me feel guilty. "Mr. Fain, I had no intention of bringing any personal trouble upon you."

"Think nothing of it. As I said, I have fought

many battles before, a good number of them in the courtroom. It is not frightening ground for me."

"I'm mighty grateful to you, Mr. Fain. I'll try to be as good a guest as I can while I'm here."

"Yes. I am afraid I will have to ask you to stay in this room. Quite dull, I know, but we simply cannot afford for you to be seen."

"I understand." I wanted to ask if I could be allowed to see Melanie, but it seemed an inappropriate question. And I also wanted to ask if he could in any way help with the search for Pa. But already he had given me more than I had any right to expect—and all for nothing more than my almost accidentally helping his daughter out of a bad situation. So I said no more.

Fain pivoted slowly on his crutches and walked toward the door. "If you have need of anything, Hop Lin will see to it. Merely knock on your door; he will be in the hall. It is his job to see to my wife, who is . . . not well." He opened the door. "Again, I repeat, if you have seen things you do not, shall we say, recognize, simply forget them. Do you understand?"

"I do."

"Good. I will wire for my attorney. In the meantime, rest well. And say nothing, nothing at all, about Jonah Littlejohn anymore. Good night." Then he closed the door.

I blew out the lamp and went to the window, looking out across the dark, flat Kansas plains, thinking over how peculiar it was that a human could feel the contradictory way I did right now: happy and grateful for hope just offered, yet terribly depressed, even sad, all at the same time.

I crawled back into bed, irritated with myself. Blast it all, I was no better than an old woman with the vapors.

By the following night, after a full day of being locked in that room with no contact beyond an occasional visit from Hop Lin, I figured no old woman had ever had a case of the vapors to match whatever I had at the moment. This was little better than being trapped in a cave. I paced about, stooping, stretching, bending, anything at all to work off my restless energy. I kept thinking about Pa, wondering if he were all right and if Primo had any reasonable chance of finding him. Perhaps I shouldn't have come here, but instead taken the risk of capture while searching for Pa myself.

I wondered again if Whitey, Potter, and Moreland might have survived the collapse of that sod house roof. It seemed unlikely, but then again, not all parts of that roof had been equally soaked and heavy. If the men lived, they might still be a threat to my father and also to me, if ever I was found.

How long would it take for Mr. Fain's attorney to arrive? What could he do for me when he did? I felt trapped and frustrated.

It took me a long time to go to sleep that night. Shortly after I did, I felt a soft touch on my shoulder and rolled over, instantly alert because of the tension coiled up inside me.

Melanie! There in my room, kneeling beside my bed. My first reaction was a burst of joy, my second a panicked fear. If Fain found his daughter here, he would probably throw off his highly cultivated, civilized manner just long enough to peel off my hair with a scalping knife. For which I wouldn't blame him; if I had a daughter like Melanie, I'd be very protective.

She was wearing a long nightgown topped by a thick woven robe. The moon through the window barely etched her beautiful face there in the darkness.

"Melanie, what are you—"

"Hush, Penn! I think I saw him!" She was distraught; tears were on her face.

"Who?"

"Jonah Littlejohn—on the street outside the house! At least, it looked like a picture of him I've seen. Penn, I think he was watching the house."

CHAPTER SEVENTEEN

"But why, Melanie?"

"He's come to cause trouble for us, maybe to hurt my father," she answered. Pausing to regather her composure, she sniffed and wiped her tears on the heel of her hand. Her midnight-black hair hung free, locks piling onto her shoulders, framing her beautiful face. "I've been afraid he would come since the letter."

"What letter? What are you talking about? Are you sure it was Mr. Littlejohn you saw?"

"Yes! Come look for yourself. Maybe he's still there." She went to the window and I followed. We looked closely into the night, and sure enough, there was a figure there. But a close inspection showed it to be the Locust Man, sauntering along through the night, waving his hands as he talked to himself.

"That's a man named Jamey Poe," I said. "That's sure not Mr. Littlejohn."

"But I swear to you, I saw Jonah Littlejohn! He

ducked back when he saw me looking down," she said despairingly. "Please believe me, Penn."

"All right. I take your word for it—though I don't see why he would take the risk of coming into town. He's suspected in a killing here. And anyway, I don't understand all of this business. What is it between Mr. Littlejohn and your family? Why is everyone so afraid of him?"

She didn't answer a few moments, struggling with her emotions. "I'm not sure it's my place to talk about it," she said finally. "Especially since I don't know exactly what you have to do with Jonah Littlejohn, either."

"I'm glad to tell you," I responded. Quickly I related to her, from the beginning, how I came to be involved with Mr. Littlejohn, what the extent of that involvement was, and wasn't. "It's just chance that our paths crossed at all. I came to Dodge to get away from a bad situation where I was living, and he came because he had some sort of business here. He never would say what it was and, once he arrived, apparently wasn't willing to do it." The next part I wasn't sure I should say, but if I wanted her to be honest with me, I would have to be honest with her. "Once I did mention the name of your father to him, and he reacted like I had cut a nerve. From then on I suspected that whatever his business in Dodge was, it had to do with Mr. Fain. But whether he wants to hurt Mr. Fain for some reason goes beyond anything I know."

"Well, I know. I'm certain he's come to hurt him, maybe kill him. And all because of her!"

"Who? Your mother?"

"Yes!" She spat out the word in a bitter whisper, then asked, after a pause, "Penn, can you love someone and still despise them sometimes?"

"That's the way I've felt sometimes about my father."

"It's that way with me for my mother. She is my mother, and I love her . . . yet sometimes I can't stand even the thought of her, much less the sight. Those ugly scars, the way she has ruined my father's life—"

Scars . . . *that* was what I had glimpsed When Hop Lin had come out of the room next door. Scars—just like those on Mr. Littlejohn's back. Now I was intrigued. I had to know more.

I said, "Melanie, what does Mr. Littlejohn have to do with all this? Won't you tell me?"

She thought about it, toying with a lock of hair.

"All right," she said.

She spoke softly, almost whispering, so that no one else in the house could hear us, and her story was fascinating.

"Most of what I can tell you I have learned from Mr. Crarie. He was not supposed to tell me these things, but he has, little by little, and I am glad he has.

"My mother's name is Marian, and once she was a beautiful woman, at least outwardly. I've been told that my father's friends warned him strongly against her when he was falling in love. She came from a poor family, but she used her beauty to advance her position.

"When Father met her, she was a show girl, working in the dance halls in St. Louis, Chicago, Louisville, but mostly on the riverboats on the Ohio and Mississippi. She performed in the riverboat gambling rooms and show halls, and perhaps did some other things best not talked about. Father was very wealthy already when she met him, and I think that is what drew her to him. It was her beauty that first attracted him, I suppose, and he fell in love with her. They announced plans to marry. It became the scandal of all my father's associations—Nigel Fain about to marry a riverboat show girl. But he didn't seem to care.

"He was deeply in love with her, but she wasn't in love with him. They tell me that even before the marriage she was unfaithful. She loved another riverboat performer, a strong man and fighter who worked all along the Mississippi. That was Jonah Littlejohn, and according to what I've heard, he had a bad reputation. There was talk that he had once killed a man and had served several years at hard labor. I suppose that might be where he developed his muscles. Mr. Crarie told me once that Jonah Littlejohn and Mother were . . . with each other the very night before the marriage. He tried to tell Father about it, to warn him away from her, but Father was stubborn. He would not listen. Father told Mr. Crarie that the marriage had already been promised, and Nigel Fain always keeps his promises, no matter what. And that is true. You know that right now firsthand, Penn, through the way Father is keeping his promise to you.

"Father and Mother were married and he took her away from the riverboats into a huge house in Cincinnati. Father liked to be close to whatever projects he was involved with at any given time, and so he moved a lot. My older brother, Francis, was born less than a year after the marriage, while Father and Mother lived in Cincinnati. But there were some, well, questions about Francis. His hair was blond, which was not a characteristic of either the Fains or my mother's family. Francis grew up to be big and muscular, and he had no interest at all in Father's work. He was born in '55, and I didn't come along until '62. I remember all the arguments between Francis and Father. They never got along. By the time I was born, Father had developed the disease that is eating away his strength bit by bit. Francis used to actually mock Father for it. He would laugh at him as his abilities slowly drained away. I hated Francis, but Mother doted on him. Cared for him much more than she ever did for me.

"Nobody who knew Mother's background ever doubted that Francis was the son of Jonah Littlejohn. Of course, nobody talked much of it beyond the usual whispers among servants and gossip in the town. I've never heard my father talk about it at all.

"Francis left home in the early seventies and headed west with a group of friends. He wanted adventure, he said. Good times. They came to Kansas in 1873 and hunted buffalo for sport, right here around Dodge, and that's when Francis was killed. There was some sort of accident during one of the hunts—he was thrown from a horse and broke his neck. They buried him out on the prairie and sent word home to Father and Mother and me. We were living then in Memphis.

"Mother all but went insane when she heard of

the death. She cut herself off from the family, moved out of Father's room and bed—would curse him when he did no more than come near her. And she would talk openly about Jonah Littlejohn and how she would find him again and leave Father forever—and Father just bore it, never shouting back, never responding in any harsh way. He loved her even when she despised him. She seemed to hold him responsible for Francis being dead, which made no sense at all. I think Father would have thrown away all his wealth and success for one indication that Mother cared about him, but she has always denied him that."

Melanie stopped for a moment, wiping her eyes. Then she went on.

"Mother ran away the next year, looking for Jonah Littlejohn. The riverboats were about gone by then, with the railroads coming in so fast, but somehow she managed to trace him down. He and a man named Priddy were putting on medicine wagon shows, and she found them somewhere in Missouri. She and Littlejohn ran off together. For all I know, they were happy together—at least, Mother must have been happy—but in Pennsylvania it all came to an end. A train they were on derailed and caught on fire when the boiler exploded. The flames reached the passenger cars, and Mother was caught in the fire.

"They say that Jonah Littlejohn could have saved her, if he had tried. But he didn't. He left her there in the fire to save himself. They say his back was badly burned as he escaped.

"But Mother had it far worse. She was burned so

terribly her hair seared off, her face, body ruined. She was nearly dead by the time they found who she was and sent word to Father and me.

"A lot of men might have turned their back on a woman who had done what Mother had, but that isn't Father's way. He went for her and brought her home. I cried for a full day when I saw what the fire had done to her. But Father hardly seemed to notice the ugliness. He loved her as much as before, maybe more.

"Yet Mother still would not love Father. She still talked only of Jonah Littlejohn, even after what he had done. Her love for that man was just as stubborn as Father's was, and is, for her.

"We came to Dodge in '78 because of Mother. Father didn't want to come, but thought it might help heal her mind, help her to adjust and accept life as it was, if she could be close to where Francis is buried. Father had this house built, moved us all out here at great inconvenience to himself—all for Mother. Yet it has seemed to make no difference to her.

"And then, right after we arrived, a letter came. It was to Mother, and it was from Jonah Littlejohn, who apparently had learned of our move to Dodge. Mother kept the letter hidden, but it dropped from her fingers once when she fell asleep in her chair, reading it alone in her room. Father found it.

"It was a strange letter, in part a history of what Littlejohn had done since he and Mother were separated, and in part sort of an apology for having left her in the flames. He said he had rejoined Priddy in a medicine show, but that it was only temporary. He was coming as soon as he could to Dodge, he said, to take Mother away from Father—no matter what was required to do it. That was the way it was worded—'no matter what is required to do it.'

"It sounded threatening to Father, and after that he has kept a close watch for Jonah Littlejohn. We had no idea he had actually come until the night you told me he was fighting on the other side of Boot Hill—that's why I reacted like I did. And then we saw in the newspapers that Mr. Littlejohn's old medicine show partner had been found murdered and that he was the suspect. We started to become more worried.

"When Father heard that you had been associated with Jonah Littlejohn some, he was concerned and suspicious about you. But I never doubted you, Penn. I knew you really had nothing seriously to do with that man.

"And that's it—that's why we're afraid of Jonah Littlejohn. And he's here, Penn. I swear to you, I saw him outside the house this very night, and I'm scared."

I was stunned by all this. So that was Jonah's business in Dodge—reuniting himself with the woman he had abandoned in a terrible situation. No wonder he so carefully hid the burn scars on his back. They must be a source of shame, like a brand marking him a coward and deserter.

"Penn, do you think he would actually try to kill Father? Is he that bad a man?"

I had no answer. I had thought I knew Jonah Littlejohn; now it was clear I really didn't.

Suddenly a loud, distorted cry came from the next room, followed by another and another. It was Melanie's mother.

Melanie leaped up and ran out the door. I got out from beneath the covers, quickly slipped on my trousers, and followed.

Melanie already was in her mother's room, and I darted in after her.

The burned woman, horrible to see by the faint flicker of the cranked-down lamp by her bed, was at the window. Tears ran down her face of ridged scars. She pointed out the window.

"It's Jonah—he's come for me—I saw him!" she said in a voice as twisted as her nearly destroyed mouth. "I knew he would come for me!"

Melanie glanced at me in a way as if to say, *I'm vindicated. I really did see Jonah Littlejohn out there.*

And then Hop Lin and Crarie were in the room with us. Crarie turned an angry glare on me.

"Get out! This is not your affair!"

"I thought she was hurt," I said. "I was trying to help."

"Your help is not needed—get out!" He angrily pointed toward the door. "Fine," I said. I went out into the hall, and Crarie slammed the door behind me.

I noticed that a lamp had been lit in the main room below, dimly lighting it. Then I saw that Nigel Fain had arisen and was trying and failing to struggle up the stairs, holding himself up on the banister. He did not have his leg braces. His bedroom was downstairs, and apparently he had dragged himself to the stairs after hearing his wife's cry, and now he

was an image of both proud determination and vain
striving as he tried to move on his own up stairs that
might as well, for him, have been a sheer cliff.

I went to him. "I'll help you, sir." He put his arm
around my shoulder and I all but carried him slowly
up the flight.

"What is it—what's happened?" he asked.

I didn't want to tell him; it did not seem my place
to do so. But he had asked and had the right to know.

"She looked out the window," I said. "She saw
someone there."

"Him?"

I swallowed, dreading to say it. "Yes."

He seemed to weaken further in my arms. "God
help me. And God help my poor Marian. Why can't
he leave us alone?"

We reached the top of the stairs. From Marian
Fain's room came the sound of babble and confusion; she was raving in that impeded voice about
Jonah Littlejohn. At that moment someone pounded
on the front door.

Fain tensed. "Oh, no."

"What do you want me to do?" I asked.

Fain was trembling, but whether from fear or fury
I could not tell. The pounding came again.

"Answer it," he commanded in a tense whisper.
"If he wants in, let him. I'll not run from him."

"Can you stand if you hold the rail, Mr. Fain?"

"Yes! Yes! Now answer!"

I helped him steady himself, then descended the
stairs. Again a heavy fist pounded the door. I
walked toward the entrance, my heart hammering.

Upstairs, Marian Fain's door opened and she

rushed out, Hop Lin right behind, trying to catch and stop her. She went past her husband as if he were not there and ran down the stairs. I froze in place, not sure now what to do.

She went past me, grabbed the door, and opened it.

Mr. Littlejohn was there; he looked down into her burn-scarred face and went white. She cried out in what sounded like a combination of joy and agony and threw her arms around him.

On the landing above, Nigel Fain collapsed.

CHAPTER EIGHTEEN

Mr. Littlejohn stared at Mrs. Fain's scarred face, the horror in his eyes unconcealed.

"Marian, is this what I left you to?" he asked her.

"I forgive you for it," she said. "I can live with it as long as I have you, Jonah." She tried to draw him closer, but he pushed her away.

"No, Marian. Don't."

"Jonah—"

Crarie, who with Hop Lin had been helping Mr. Fain back to his feet, came bounding down the stairs and went to a desk in the corner of the room. From a drawer he withdrew a small pistol and leveled it at Mr. Littlejohn:

"You, sir, may consider yourself a prisoner. You will do no harm here," Crarie said. His posture with the pistol was that of a fencer—spread-legged, weapon arm forward, the other back. I wondered if Crarie had ever handled a pistol before; I rather doubted it, judging from appearances.

Mr. Littlejohn looked at Crarie as if his words had been in some unknown language, failing to register. He looked back at Mrs. Fain and, though he tried to hide it, shuddered. He pushed her away to arm's length.

"Jonah! Don't do this to me, you can't!"

"Now is not the time for this, Marian," he said. "There's a more important reason I'm here."

"More important? What do you mean? You came for me, like you wrote you would! There's nothing more important!"

He backed away from her. "No. Things have to be different, Marian. How can you even want me, anyway, after what I did? Don't you see me for what I am? You don't belong with me. You never did."

Marian Fain cried loudly. "It's my scars—you hate me because I'm ugly!"

"It isn't your scars that bother me, Marian. It's mine. God knows how many times I've wished they were anywhere but on my back—on my arms, my face, anywhere would be better than where they are, because every time I feel them, see them, I know they are where they are because I turned my back on you when you needed me. That's why you don't belong with me, Marian. You belong with the man who loves you, your husband."

The scarred woman was speechless. Her arms fell to her sides and she backed into the room and sank into a soft chair. Her fire-gnarled hands rose to her face and she cried.

"But you love me, Jonah!"

He shook his head. "I'm sorry, Marian. I don't. I never did. Maybe I thought I did at one time, but a man doesn't love someone he leaves to burn. If you'd think about that, you'd see it."

Then Mr. Littlejohn looked at me. "It's you I've come for, Penn," he said.

"Sir," Crarie called to Mr. Fain, "shall I drop him where he stands?"

"Put the pistol down, Mr. Crarie," Fain returned. He was on his feet again, holding onto the rail. "There will be no violence here."

Crarie lowered the pistol, but retained it.

"You came for me?" I asked. "What do you mean?"

"Your father is out there on the prairie, waiting for you. Primo Smith found us; he's with him."

My mind flashed back to Moreland's conversation in the dugout, his talk of Pa having someone with him. I never would have thought it would be Mr. Littlejohn.

"Come on; let's go," he said. "Your pa is waiting."

I ran back up the stairs and into my room, where I put on my shirt. Hop Lin had washed it today; it felt crisp and good on my back and shoulders. Pa, out there waiting for me; I couldn't believe it. I was like a little boy at Christmas. My talk to myself about having put Pa aside, about not caring about him because he no longer cared about me—all that was gone now. Pa was there, and I was going to him.

When I got back downstairs, Mr. Littlejohn was talking again, very intensely, to Mrs. Fain, who was crying all the harder. Nigel Fain's face bore an expression I hope never to see again on a human face; I wondered what feelings he must have, watching the wife he loved so much go on as she was because her former lover would have nothing of her now.

Melanie came to me and touched me. "Be careful," she urged in a whisper.

"I'm going to my Pa," I said. It was all I could think about; caution, other concerns no longer pertained.

Out on the porch, Mr. Littlejohn closed the door behind us. For a moment he bent over, hands on his knees, and breathed like he had just completed a long run. Obviously the encounter in the house had been hard for him.

"I don't understand why you came," I said. "Why didn't you just send Primo back for me?"

"I had to do this myself," he said. "I had to walk in that house and resolve things. We've got long history, that family and me."

"I heard about it, from Melanie. Was that the business you came to Dodge for—to tell Mrs. Fain you had to let her go?"

"No. It was the opposite at first. I came to Dodge to take her away from him. Felt I owed it to her for what I did. Did the girl tell you about that, too?"

"Yes."

"I hate for you even to know it. It's a shameful thing, like these scars I carry."

"The Fains are frightened of you, Mr. Littlejohn. They think you are a very bad man."

"They're right. I am a very bad man. Always have been. Afraid I always will be because I hear tell there's few second chances. Come on—if we're seen dawdling here we'll wind up in the lime kiln instead of with your father."

He had two horses waiting. His, I figured, he probably had stolen the night he fled Dodge. The other might have been stolen, too, or maybe it was

Pa's. We made a wide swing northeast around town, figuring we had less chance of being seen that way. We circled Boot Hill and the adjacent rise, then cut around past the houses on Military Avenue and made for the open plains.

When we were out on the plains, I asked, "Mr. Littlejohn, did you kill Winfred Priddy like they say?"

"I did. He came at me with a knife and I had to do it."

"They may not believe that. They're liable to put you away for it. Maybe execute you. Word's out to look for you."

"We'll worry about all that when this is done. Right now the thing to do is get you to your Pa. He needs to see you. He's a sick man, and he's been looking for you."

We rode until time didn't matter and I had lost track of distance. The horses traveled well in the cool night. Near Fort Dodge we forded the river and headed south. We were on the barren flats now, riding easily along. We stopped to spell and water the horses at a little creek, then went on, hardly speaking.

We were still riding when the sun came up and sent our shadows stretching toward Colorado. Finally we came upon a little creek and Mr. Littlejohn reined to a stop.

"There we'll find him, Penn." He pointed toward a place where the creek ran beneath a rocky bank. I saw nothing at first, but when we drew closer, there was one of Primo's mules grazing by the water. The bank was concave, making a rocky overhang beside the water.

Primo knelt there, and when we came near he stood and waved. I waved back, and then I saw Pa near him.

He was lying in blankets beneath the overhang, and even across the distance in the thin morning light he looked bad. Dread and anticipation merged as a dry lump in my throat.

We splashed across the creek and rode in.

Pa cried when I came to him and threw his arms around my shoulders and made me cry, too. He looked older and weaker, not the man he was. When his tears were cried out, he looked me over and smiled.

"Penn, son, I've run through this moment in my mind a thousand times, but the real meeting is better than the imagined one. I've missed you for a long time, son."

"I've missed you too, Pa," I said, and didn't realize until I had said it just how true it was.

Primo and Mr. Littlejohn mounted and went off for a ride to give Pa and me some privacy. The two of us got reacquainted as best we could under the circumstances, and I briefly told him what had happened to me these past years, right on up through my capture by Moreland and his other old prison mates.

"I didn't believe them when they said you had been free, Pa. I told them you would have come to me when you got out."

He looked guiltily toward the ground. "Shame is a powerful force, Penn. I couldn't come back to you empty-handed. That's why I didn't let you know at once."

"Is shame why you never answered my letters?" I felt a twinge of familiar bitterness.

"Yes. You may not understand that, but it's true. A man who looks down on himself like I came to do in that prison feels his son would be best off forgetting him. But now you can be proud of me again, Penn. I brought you something that will make up for the lost time, and all I didn't give you before." He reached beneath his shirt and brought out a sealed envelope of brown paper, bent to the shape of him, warmed and worn by long wearing close to his body.

"What's this?"

"An honest-to-goodness treasure map, Penn. Tells you where you can find enough wealth to keep you happy long after I'm gone."

"Gone?"

His smile died away. "Look at me. I'm a dying man. I been sick since shortly after they locked me up. Something bad wrong in here, and getting worse. They say there's nothing to be done." He pounded his lungs with the flat side of a fist.

"No, Pa. Don't say that."

"It's true, and there's no point denying it or weeping over it. I'd rather live, sure, but if I can't, then I have to do what I can to make sure you're all right for money."

"I don't want money. I want you. You're all I ever wanted."

"Don't, Penn. Listen to me. There's gold hidden away for you, and what's in that envelope tells you where to find it. Enough money to set you up anywhere you please, doing what you want. Enough for you to find a little lady and marry and have your own ranch or farm or store. It's my legacy to you, Penn."

I had an empty space inside that seemed to be getting bigger as Pa talked. "Where did you get gold, Pa? And if you got it, why do you have to hide it?"

"That's Colorado gold I'm talking about. Pikes Peak gold, high-graded a long time ago and hid away. I learned where it was while I was in prison. Once it was Moreland's, but he took sick in prison, thought he was about to die, and I convinced him to tell me, saying he should make a clean breast before he died, and such as that." Pa grinned. "Men will listen to a lot at times like that they won't listen to otherwise. Anyway, when he told me where the gold was, I knew right then I finally had something worthwhile to give you, Penn."

This was getting bad, bad. I could almost have cried again, and this time not for happiness.

Pa kept talking. "Ironic part is, Moreland never died. He got well instead and was after me right off, since I knew about his gold. It took some careful tricking around, but I was able to set him up to be blamed for some trouble in the prison that got him a longer sentence and me a shortened one. I left Moreland in there and went after that gold. Found it, too, and rehid it. That paper you got is the only record of where it can be found."

"Moreland wants his gold back, Pa," I said. "That's why he captured me—I think he wanted to use me to force you to turn it back over. What you're calling your legacy to me just about got me killed."

"But Primo said Moreland and them got crushed under a wet sod house roof. So you don't need to worry now, huh?"

Pa didn't seem to be getting my point at all. It was depressing. "Yeah. No need to worry," I said. "If Moreland's dead, that is. I didn't hang around to check."

"He's dead, I'll bet. Man can't cheat the reaper twice. Still, be careful. That envelope is valuable, Penn. A lot of folks, if they found out what it is, would want it."

I stuck it back at him. "Let them have it, then. I don't want it."

Pa looked at me in disbelief. "What do you mean, don't want it?"

"Just that. I didn't come here to have you give me a bunch of stolen gold. I came to get my father, not money."

Pa's expression went black. He dug under his blanket and came out with a bottle. He took a long swallow and wiped his mouth on his sleeve. A long coughing spell followed, and I could tell it hurt him. He turned bleary, angry eyes to me.

"Stubborn little ranny, you are. Stubborn as sin, just like your sorry mother. Man goes to any length of trouble for you, and you throw it back in his face. What kind of son are you, anyway?"

"Just a son who wanted his father, not just things his father could, or couldn't, give him."

Our argument might have gotten a lot worse then, but something happened that cut it short. A rifle cracked out on the plains, and a bullet splatted into the bank above our heads.

"What in the name—" Pa started to say, sitting up in his blankets.

"Get down, Pa," I ordered. "Get down low—that's Moreland out there."

Moreland it was, and he now ran due west, dropping in a little gully. He aimed, fired again, and a bullet thudded the ground about a yard to our left.

"Down, Pa! Before he pins down his aim on us."

I had to all but drag Pa down flat. I bunched his blanket up before us so Moreland would have trouble seeing us.

Moreland's shout reached us: "Worth, this ain't how I planned to do this! We were going to come at you with a gun at your boy's head, but that didn't quite work out, so we're forced to take a more direct approach. We're going to plug the life out of you unless you give me word right now where you've put my gold!"

"Ain't your gold!" Pa yelled back. "You murdered the old man who high-graded it, and you know it! It's fair game to whoever's got it! Besides, there's four of us together here—that shot probably has already brought the other two back this way!"

"There's four of us out here, too!" Moreland yelled back. "And one of them's Potter, and he shoots good enough to count for two or three by himself! Spano and Whitey are here too. I'm taking you with me, Worth—you're going to lead me to that gold before you up and die and I lose it."

"Pa, I don't believe anybody but Moreland's out there," I said. "I doubt they all survived that collapsed roof. And I *know* he's lying about Spano—

he'd have died from snakebite even without the roof falling on him."

Pa listened to me, then yelled, "You're bluffing, Moreland! My boy here says the others are dead!"

Moreland paused. "You in there, boy?"

"I am!" I shouted back.

"You left me to die under that mud roof, boy!"

"You'd have been no deader than three people you murdered in Eldridge!" I returned. "If you got any friends out there, let them raise a yell themselves!"

Silence on the prairie. Moreland obviously had not known I was here; if he had he wouldn't have tried a bluff he knew I could see straight through. Now he was in a bind.

"I'm doing the talking here, not anybody else!" Moreland shouted back. There was a touch of panic in his voice.

"Why'd you take such a chance on so fool a bluff as this?" Pa shouted, then collapsed into a fit of harsh coughing. The yelling was hard on him.

"You're a dying man, Worth! I . . . we couldn't afford to wait any longer."

"I'll see you dead before you get that gold, Moreland."

Moreland fired again; this time the shot came closer.

"I sure wish Primo and Mr. Littlejohn would get back," I said. "They couldn't have ridden far."

Pa was getting mad. "You get out of here, Moreland—you're asking to die if you stay around here."

Moreland fired again, and this shot almost hit me.

Another shot came in response. I looked straight

up; over the edge of the overhang above me, Primo's hands thrust out, holding a rifle. He fired one more shot that kicked up the dirt in front of Moreland, who was flat in a little gully. The second shot must have at least nicked Moreland, for he yelled and jumped up to run for better cover. Had he merely kept running he might have been all right; instead he raised his rifle and fired back at us. The shot went high, but it prompted Primo to fire again, and Moreland jerked and collapsed, moved on the ground, then lay still.

Pa leaped up with surprising vigor for a sick man. He came out from under the overhang and stuck his hand up toward Primo. "Let me shake your hand, Mr. Smith," he said. "That was some fine shooting."

Primo did not shake the hand. He stood and walked around and down to where we were. He looked grim indeed, and stared across at Moreland's body.

"I take no pleasure in killing," he said. "I had done nary of it since Adobe Walls, and I had hoped never to have to again."

"Moreland ain't worth worrying over," Pa said, grinning. He coughed hard and the pain took the grin away.

Primo turned his back. Pa shrugged and started walking across to examine Moreland's body.

"You saved our lives, Primo," I said. "Thanks." I looked around. "Where's Mr. Littlejohn?"

"Gone."

"Where to?"

"Don't know. He said he had to talk some more to somebody—something like that. He just rode on."

So he had gone back to Dodge, to the Fain house, no doubt. I didn't feel good about that; it appeared to me that whatever talking needed to be done with the Fains had been done when Mr. Littlejohn came to get me. If he indeed was going back to Dodge, he was running quite a risk of being captured by the law.

"You have a good reunion with your father?" Primo asked.

I looked across at Pa, who had just reached Moreland's body and was bending over it.

"Truth is, Primo, we sort of—"

Moreland's right hand came up, gripping a pistol. He shot Pa through the forehead as I watched, and Pa fell atop him.

CHAPTER NINETEEN

Moreland's murder of Pa was the final act of his life. He died with Pa's corpse on top of him; by the time Primo and I reached them, both were dead.

I grieved in silence over Pa for a time, and then Primo came to me and put his arm on my shoulder.

"Penn, let's get your father's body back to Dodge. Then let's you and me go talk to Bat, if he's there. I think maybe we should have done that right off—the longer we wait, the worse it seems to get."

He was right. It struck me how wrong I had been about Primo; back when I first met him I had thought him not too intelligent. Now he seemed to be the wisest, most capable man I had known in a long time.

We cut dragpoles from some trees beside the little creek and made a litter from Pa's blankets. I wrapped his body in another blanket and stitched it closed, then tied Pa's already stiffening form onto the litter.

As for Moreland, we left his body where it fell. His corpse didn't deserve burial, in our estimation.

Pa's death had drained my spirit; they could have scheduled a hanging for me right then and I would have pitched in to help build the gallows. In any case, I was tired of running and actually eager to talk to Bat Masterson. I would go back and face whatever I found, and Nigel Fain's attorney could help me.

We rode slowly and stopped twice to let the mounts rest and graze.

A couple of miles short of Fort Dodge, Primo started talking quietly. He told me how he had found Pa and Mr. Littlejohn together by the creek. Mr. Littlejohn apparently had run across Pa accidentally, and Pa had thrown down on him with a gun. That had forced Mr. Littlejohn to do a lot of talking and explaining to save his own skin. Somehow my name had come out, and Pa had revealed himself for who he was. Mr. Littlejohn had stuck close to Pa after that, for he had seen the sickness in him and knew he needed care. Besides, Mr. Littlejohn had some healing of his own to begin, what with his whipping injuries. Moreland must have come along unseen during that time, seen Mr. Littlejohn with Pa, and gone out to the dugout where I was prisoner to report to his companions.

Shortly after, Primo had begun his own search, found Mr. Littlejohn and Pa, and told them what had happened to me and that I was hiding at the Fain house.

Mr. Littlejohn, Primo said, had insisted on being the one to return to Dodge to get me, once he found out I was with the Fains. Primo had argued against it, saying he should go instead since the law wasn't after him, but Mr. Littlejohn had been adamant and ridden off before the argument could be settled.

"He had reasons for going to the Fains beyond just getting me," I said. "I'll tell you about it sometime—it's a long story."

When we neared Dodge, Primo asked, "Are you sure you want to do this? After all, it's your neck, not mine. Maybe we could cut around and get you to the Fain place without you being seen. You could still hide out awhile if you think it best."

"No. I'm turning myself in. I'm weary of all this dodging and hiding, and it only makes me look more guilty, anyway."

Primo nodded approvingly. "You're a right courageous young fellow, Penn."

We drew a lot of attention when we rode down Front Street, Pa's covered body dragging behind on the litter. As people began figuring out who I was, I could see their interest heighten even more. Apparently the name of Penn Malone had been thrown around a lot since news of the murders in Eldridge. I would have felt self-conscious and angry a bit earlier to have felt their stares and known what they were thinking of me, but now I didn't care. Pa was gone, his attempts to heal old wounds with stolen gold had miserably failed, and the world was a bleak place for me.

Only one bright spot existed in it: Melanie Fain. Yet I did not yet know exactly how I stood even with her.

A crowd slowly gathered as we pulled to a stop near the First Avenue intersection. Those who recognized me looked at me like I was a rattler that had bitten a baby; they looked at Primo like he was loco to be still associating with me.

"Who's the dead man?" somebody asked.

"That's his pa," Primo said.

"What—he kill him, too?"

I should have been angry enough at that to react with a fist or at least a retort, but I felt nothing. I was as lifeless as those Dull Knife raiders I had seen on the steps of the courthouse the day Masterson had paid his visit to Dan Johnson's.

Thinking of Masterson . . . there he was, riding up the street in that buggy he used to traverse the huge area he had to cover. He looked dressed to travel today, but when he saw the crowd, he drove over, braked, and climbed out.

The crowd parted to let him through. By now Charlie Bassett and Wyatt Earp had also appeared.

I turned to Masterson, whom I felt I knew best. "Sheriff, I'm turning myself in to you. My pa was killed before my eyes, right now I don't much care what happens, I'm tired to my soul of hiding—so you do with me what you want."

He peeked inside the blanket at Pa's dead face, then pushed his hat back on his head with the tip of his cane.

"Penn, I got a wire this morning from Eldridge. Seems they found a witness that said he saw the men who did those killings. Three of them, in long coats. You're not a suspect anymore."

The people gathered about shot looks all around and murmured in surprise, but none was more surprised than me.

"You mean they aren't blaming me anymore?"

"That's what I said."

Tremendous relief swept over me. I could have laughed, cried, and danced all at once, but then Pa's death nudged its ugly presence into my thoughts again and my joy slowly choked away.

"What happened to your father?" Earp asked.

"He was shot by a partner of the three who did the Eldridge killings. You'll find him dead a few miles southeast of Fort Dodge, by the creek. His name is Moreland. The other three are crushed under the roof of a fallen-in sod house west of here. Their names are Pete Spano, Potter Griggs, and Whitey something-or-other."

All that brought new murmurs and exclamations.

"Maybe we better take Mr. Malone in for a talk," Earp said to Masterson, who nodded. "Primo, you come along too, huh? Charlie, think you can get this body off the street and to the coroner?"

Bassett nodded. I dismounted and handed him the reins.

Masterson said, "See to my buggy, too, if you would, Charlie." Then to the rest of us: "We might as well talk where we can be comfortable." He led me, Primo, and Earp toward the Long Branch, and the crowd fell in behind. Masterson turned. "You folks head back to your own business," he directed, and they did.

*　*　*

The rest of the day was something of a blur for me. When it was done, I remembered mostly having talked, talked, talked some more—telling my story in intricate detail, going back over it when it wasn't clear, and finally having the satisfaction of knowing that these peace officers fully understood me. And better still, believed me.

Primo talked too, describing his part in finding Pa and how he had shot Moreland and Moreland had shot Pa. In the process, he mentioned Mr. Littlejohn, obviously before he thought much about that. The mention drew a burst of questions from the officers, and after some hesitation Primo opened up and spoke freely and truthfully, and I did the same, mentioning that Mr. Littlejohn had told me the killing of Priddy had been in self-defense. Of Mr. Littlejohn's affairs with the Fains, though, I said nothing.

"He told me that Winfred Priddy came at him first," I said.

"I don't doubt it," Masterson said. "There's at least two score witnesses who saw Priddy go after him with a bullwhip after that fight. And old Jamey Poe—you may have heard him called the Locust Man—swears he witnessed the killing, and that Priddy really did go after Littlejohn first. Jamey may not seem much of a reliable witness, but under the circumstances I believe him, and I think a jury might, too. Especially if you also testified on Mr. Littlejohn's behalf, Penn, and told them what he told you."

Hearing that made me feel better about having talked about him to the law, but it also gave me a strong feeling of irony: Mr. Littlejohn was running for fear of a murder charge he might never face at all.

"I'll start gathering a posse, Bat," Earp said. "He's probably close by."

When the talking was done, Primo and I went back to the dugout. I had intended to stop on the way at the Fain house and tell Mr. Fain what had happened, but I was so weary in mind and body I decided to put it off. Primo and I went on to the dugout for some rest. All the while I wondered where Mr. Littlejohn was.

The despairing Marian Fain set her house on fire a couple of hours past sunset, when I had just stirred from a long afternoon of sleep. On the street I heard a couple of yells, the sound of a running horse and pounding feet, then the sound of a fire engine bell.

I leaped to my feet, pulled on pants, shirt, and boots, and ran out the door.

Primo was already out there. "Look yonder," he said, pointing.

From where we were I could tell it was the Fain house.

"Melanie . . ." I took off running. Primo ran too, but I left him far behind.

The Dodge City Fire Company was already at work when I got there. I ran straight for the house, but one of the firemen stepped in my way.

"Hold on there, young fellow. You leave this to us."

"But Melanie is—"

"I'm here, Penn!" It was Melanie's voice. I turned; she came to me and put her arms around me.

"What happened?"

"She did it . . . set fire in the upper hall." Melanie's voice quaked with emotion. "She's been in such a despair over Jonah Littlejohn. I think she's trying to finish what didn't get finished when that train burned—trying to kill herself. She's still in there. But at least Father is—" She stopped. "Father! Penn, where is he?"

I looked around; Fain was not to be seen.

"He was here a moment ago. . . . They dragged him out . . ."

"Oh, no," I said. Her gaze followed mine.

Nigel Fain's brace-bound form was silhouetted in the door of the burning house. He had managed to move around the edge of the crowd and make it onto the porch before being noticed. Now he vanished inside.

"Hey, hey you!" one of the firemen shouted. He ran after Mr. Fain, went inside.

The upper level of the house was filling with fire; it leaped out the windows. Through the open front door I saw the staircase starting to burn. Nigel Fain was trying to go up it, but the fireman reached him. They seemed to struggle, and then something big and burning crashed down from above and hid them. A woman near me, who had a similar angle of view and thus also had seen it happen, screamed.

I broke away from Melanie and darted past the firemen who had restrained me before. They shouted at me, one came after me, but I was too fast. Before I even had thought about what I was doing, I was inside the blazing building.

The smoke was thick and growing thicker, the

heat incredible. I squinted and put my hand over my mouth and nose and tried to see.

There . . . on the staircase. Mr. Fain was moving, struggling upward one hot step at a time like an infant too young to really crawl. The fireman who had gone after him lay dead beneath the flaming beam that had fallen on him.

A woman screamed upstairs, again and again. Marian Fain was still alive, and now, from the sound of her, had changed her mind about wanting to burn to death.

Behind me more flaming timbers fell; the living room was filling with fire.

I knew what Fain was doing: trying to reach his wife. But it was clearly futile for him.

"Mr. Fain—it's no use!" I shouted into his ear. "Let me get you out!"

"Got to get to her—"

"Leave her to me, Mr. Fain—save yourself!"

But he was beyond reason, moved by pure instinct to protect the one he loved. He pushed me down; I fell back down the stairs and almost landed atop the burning timber that had crushed the fireman.

I had seen no one else enter the house yet; probably everyone had written both of us off after the new timbers had fallen behind us. I could imagine the despair Melanie must be suffering right now. I found myself hoping she worried almost as much for me as for her parents—it was an odd thought that told me I truly was in love with her. I tucked it away in my mind for later pondering—if there was to be a later.

Fire was coming down the stairs toward Mr. Fain,

all but rolling like a ball. "No!" I screamed. "No!"—and went after him again.

The heat-weakened stair collapsed beneath us; we tumbled together into the dark closet below. My head struck something; I almost lost consciousness—almost.

I retained enough awareness to see the door open a moment later and feel the big arms that swept down to pull me from the smoke-filled closet.

"I got you, boy, I got you," Mr. Littlejohn said as he pulled me from the closet. Where he had come from I didn't know. I went over his shoulder like a sack of grain, and all I knew was that I was moving through what I thought surely was hell itself—flame, smoke, unbearable heat, air that was like acid in the lungs.

I may have passed out then for a few moments, for what I next realized was lying on the ground, my head on Melanie's lap. I was coughing harder than I had ever coughed.

"Look, Penn, look!" Melanie said in an awed voice. Then, louder and joyfully: "He's got him out—look, Penn!"

I did look, and saw Mr. Littlejohn carry Nigel Fain out the front door, down the steps, the house burning behind him. He had, incredibly, weaved a safe path through the flaming front room.

The crowd cheered. Applauded. The strong man who had told me he hated crowds had just performed the greatest feat of his career so far, and the crowd adored it.

He brought Mr. Fain down to where I was. I sat up as Melanie went to the crippled man and cradled him in her arms.

Fain twisted his head and looked at Mr. Littlejohn. "Marian . . ." he whispered. "Still inside."

"Where?" Mr. Littlejohn asked.

"Upstairs."

Mr. Littlejohn rose, looking into the hellish flame. "Are there back stairs?"

"Yes . . . through the back door," Fain responded.

I tried to come to my feet, but fell back. I could hardly breathe, and my voice all but croaked. "Don't do it, Mr. Littlejohn," I said. "Let the fireman go for her." Yet they were not going.

He still stared into the fire; his face was orange and yellow in its light. This was a man who knew in his own flesh the pain fire could bring; I could see the battle within him.

"No. This time I don't leave her to burn," he said, not to me or Fain or Melanie, but to himself.

Just then several people converged on him to praise him for what he had done, but he pushed them off like Samson toppling those pillars in the Bible story. He stepped forward.

"No sir—you've got out your last one," one of the fireman said, grasping Mr. Littlejohn's shoulder. "That lady is gone. You can't even hear her screaming no more."

Mr. Littlejohn turned and put his fist into the man's jaw. If I had had more of a voice I might have cheered; the fireman's callous comment had been made in full hearing of Melanie and Mr. Fain.

Mr. Littlejohn pushed on past and circled the house. He disappeared around the back, and I all but knew when he did that I would see him no more, that the flames would eat him alive.

Then, for a long time, there was nothing but roaring flame, steadily leaping higher, the firemen working, the people crowding in too close and being forced back again and again by the fire crew. . . .

Melanie screamed and pointed toward an upper window.

It was unbelievable, almost miraculous, but there he was. Mr. Littlejohn's big form leaned out of a second-story window that had blown out its glass from heat long before. In his arms was the limp body of Marian Fain, the clothes burned from her, her pitifully scarred body exposed.

"Catch her! Catch her!" he shouted.

The firemen, stunned for a moment into statues just like the rest of us, moved forward, near the heat-belching house, and extended a score of arms.

Mr. Littlejohn threw her, screaming at the same time, for he was on fire.

They caught her, brought her back. I heard voices in a rapid jumble: She's burned, look at the burns, no—those are scars, who is this woman? What happened to her?

Behind me Mr. Fain cried with joy, for she was alive. Alive, and she had not suffered many fresh burns; she apparently had reached some protective corner where Mr. Littlejohn had found her.

I was staring numbly up at the window where I had seen him last. He was no longer there. The house was engulfed now. No hope.

I bowed my head and prayed for Jonah Littlejohn—that his death had not been too painful, and that somehow all was well with him now.

CHAPTER TWENTY

But he hadn't died at all. Death for Jonah Littlejohn would not come until hours later.

Jamey Poe spent those hours with his nose pressed to the window of the room where they carried Mr. Littlejohn after Jamey found him sheltered beneath the few unburnt timbers in what remained of Nigel Fain's house. Jamey had run shouting that he was alive, by heaven, alive—all burnt up like a locust down a chimney but still alive, believe it or not.

We didn't believe it when we heard it, but Jamey screamed it again and again until he drew us over and showed us that he spoke the truth.

Before I actually saw the injured husk of Mr. Littlejohn there under the dawn sky, I was glad he had lived. It was a miracle, I believed. Then I saw him, and believed that no longer. This was no miracle, but a curse, the same one that had kept Marian Fain alive after her own burning in that train long before. The burnt, stinking thing that remained of Mr. Littlejohn did not look like it could be alive, and yet the chest rose up and down, again and again, life clinging like a scared child to its mother.

How can he bear the pain? I thought. How is it he isn't screaming, begging to die? But he did not scream. He did not even moan as he was carried on a litter improvised from an old door to a nearby house.

There was nothing to be done for him, and everyone knew it. As the morning went on, a crowd lingered on the porch, waiting for word of the strongman's death. But inside, Mr. Littlejohn lingered, and eventually the group of stragglers drifted apart, dissolving slowly as a cloud. By afternoon, which turned leaden and cloudy, there remained only two of us at vigil: Jamey outside at the window, me at the bedside. Jamey was unwilling to enter the house but also unwilling to leave it, so he stood peering through the window like a child at a storefront.

I prayed for Mr. Littlejohn. Lord, I implored, don't let his suffering continue. Show him whatever mercies you can. I know little of such things; I just ask that you show him mercy.

When I lifted my head, Mr. Littlejohn was looking at me, bloodshot eyes with the dull glimmer of unpolished marbles in his blackened face.

The sheet I had covered him with had slipped down, revealing his fire-eaten arms that had drawn up to him as if he were about to begin one last saloon fight. I reached for the sheet and pulled it up to cover his arms again.

"No."

I couldn't believe he had actually spoken. Maybe it was just a ghost of a voice, not a full-throated one—but a voice it was. I got up from my chair and knelt beside the bed. I wanted to take one of the twisted hands in mine, but feared it would only make him hurt more.

"But you shouldn't have to look at . . . at yourself," I said.

"Want to look. I want to."

I didn't understand that, but I nodded.

"Is she alive?" he asked.

"Yes," I said. "You saved her."

It might have been a wince of suffering, but I think he smiled then. "This time . . . I didn't fail her," he said in that coarse whisper-voice.

"No. You didn't fail her."

"Didn't run out on her like I did on that train." His eyes shifted down and he studied his burnt hands. "Look at them, Penn. Burns on my hands this time, not my back. The way it should have been before."

I tried to say something, but my voice was lost somewhere in my tight throat.

"Proud of those burns," he said, his voice even more a whisper than before. His eyes closed, and I think maybe he smiled one more time, and then it was just me at the bedside and Jamey Poe at the window, and on the bed a blackened form that used to be a man, but wasn't anymore.

I stood by his grave, my hat in my hands, and Melanie came quietly to me. Scuffing my toe in the freshly turned pile of dirt, I blinked back a tear, for I did not want her to see me cry. Not that she would have thought it bad or shameful; it was just the way I had been raised. When a man felt like I did right now, he didn't show it.

Melanie touched my arm. "I'm glad he died thinking he had saved her," she said. I had told her of Mr. Littlejohn's last hours, which unknown to me at the time, had also been the last hours of Marian Fain. Her injuries had proven too much for her, and she had quietly passed on, perhaps ironically or perhaps appropriately, at almost the same moment he had.

"He did save her," I said. "She lived, at least for a time, because of what he did."

"And she also died because of him, in a way," Melanie said, but there was no bitterness in it. Both of us, I think, were mostly drained of feeling right now. Not much remained inside us but the remnants of grief, and in me, a desire to turn away from it all and run as hard, fast, and far as I could.

"Are you still planning to leave?" she asked. I could tell it wasn't a comfortable question for her.

"I've got to," I said. "Can't stay here any longer. What about you?"

"I'll go wherever my father wants to go," she said. She hesitated a moment, then added, "I had hoped that maybe you would want to—" She broke off.

I knew what she would have said: that I would want to come with her and Nigel Fain. And in my heart I did. I did not at all want to leave her—yet I couldn't stay. At the moment I didn't feel I had a choice, if I wanted to keep my sanity.

Perhaps Melanie understood that, or perhaps she

simply saw that further words were futile, for she said nothing else as she turned and walked away, leaving me alone beside Jonah Littlejohn's grave.

I felt the tiny flicker of an urge to go after her and tell her I would stay after all, but the flicker died, and I remained where I was, staring down at the mound of settling earth.

I said goodbye to no one before I left, riding a fine horse that Nigel Fain had given me. Melanie had told him of my plan to leave. He had vowed to me earlier to help me in whatever way I needed; this, I suppose, was just one more way he was keeping that vow. He said nothing about it when he gave me the horse, but I sensed he did not want me to leave any more than Melanie did.

I left anyway, thinking to depart Kansas forever. It seemed that Kansas held only loss and pain for me. Here I had lost Pa, Mr. Littlejohn, Mr. Ramm . . . and now Melanie, most likely. Mr. Fain had nothing to keep him in Dodge now, and surely he would leave it. Melanie would go with him. Maybe go off so far I could not find her again. The thought burned, yet still I did not turn around.

That night, on the plains miles from Dodge, I slept like a stone, weary to the deepest part of my soul. I awakened suddenly; the sun had just edged over the eastern horizon.

What had awakened me was the sound of a distant wagon, coming from the east out of the sun. I stood, hearing it long before I saw it. When I did see it, a cold shiver ran down my back, even colder than the one I had felt when first I saw Primo on his bone wagon.

It was a medicine show wagon, much like Mr. Littlejohn's. Closer it came, creaking and squeaking. Then another sound reached me: a voice, thin and female, making music. A young woman, it sounded like, singing. The voice wasn't beautiful, but haunting, and the song was an eerie-sounding ballad I had never heard before. That cold shiver came again.

I straightened my rumpled clothing and walked nearer the road, watching the wagon approach. By now I could make out a figure in the driver's seat. It was a man with a long blond beard. At first I couldn't see the girl, but then I spotted her atop the wagon. She was facing toward the east, looking into the sunrise, her legs dangling over the rear of the wagon top. Her music was more audible. There was something familiar in all of this, something beyond mere similarity between this wagon and that of Priddy and Littlejohn.

The bearded driver touched his hat and grinned broadly at me as the wagon swept on past. M. N. SMYTH'S TRAVELING SHOWCASE, tall painted letters on the side of the wagon said. There was more, but I didn't have time to read it. At this distance I could tell that the wagon was brand new.

When it was past, I finally saw the young woman's face, just as she waved at me, still singing, kicking her legs like a child splashing her toes in a spring.

I couldn't help but laugh aloud.

Dixie Trimble must have enjoyed her brief stint with Priddy's medicine show, for obviously she had taken up quickly with a new one. And apparently the medicine show life was doing her well. Dixie was still delicate, still pale and frail, but somehow much more alive than ever I had seen her. Before she had carried an aura of illness, of sickrooms with heavy drawn curtains, of medicines and tonics and tombstones. Now, sitting in the morning sun atop that wagon, singing in a thin but clear voice, she seemed as renewed as springtime.

It struck me that maybe Dixie had experienced a sort of resurrection after all. But something else struck me more forcefully still.

On the back of the wagon, beneath Dixie's swinging feet, was a little scrap of verse, no doubt excerpted from one of her poems. I read it as the wagon receded, and it stayed with me the next two hours as I struggled to continue my journey away from Dodge. At last I pulled up short, turned my mount, and looked back the way I had come.

Aloud I recited:

> Hold dear your days;
> They're too soon flown,
> And second chances seldom come.

I shook my head, smiling at myself, wondering why I was so slow to learn.

My father had sought a second chance and failed to find it. Jonah Littlejohn had sought one as well, and it had been given to him. Painfully, fatally—but it had been given, and that was all he had wanted.

Now I had my own second chance to live, and she was not ahead, but back in Dodge. The past was gone, the future was not yet, and in the present I did have a choice after all, and in half a moment I made it.

Spurring my horse, I rode back toward Dodge, the sunrise on my back and my shadow stretching westward before me.

A NOTE FROM THE AUTHOR

I was born in 1956 in Cookeville, Tennessee, and I remain a resident Tennessean. I wrote my first Western at age twenty-two.

My interest in the American West is just part of a broader interest in the frontier. I am fascinated by the vast westward expanses on the other side of the Mississippi, but I am equally intrigued by the original American West: the area west of the Appalachians and east of the Mississippi. I hope someday to write fiction set in that older frontier at the time of its settlement, in addition to traditional Westerns.

My interest in Westerns was sparked in early childhood by television, movies, and books. I appreciate both the fact of the West and the myth of the West; and I believe both aspects have a valid place in popular fiction.

I received an undergraduate degree in English and journalism, plus teaching accreditation in English and history, from Tennessee Technological University in 1979. Since that time I have been a newspaperman by profession, both as a writer and an editor. Today I am on the editorial staff of the daily newspaper in Greeneville, Tennessee, one of the state's most historic towns.

Greeneville is the seat of the county that contributed one of America's original frontier heroes to the world—Davy Crockett. Greeneville was also the hometown of President Andrew Johnson and was for several years the capital of the Lost State of Franklin—an eighteenth-century political experiment that came close to achieving statehood.

I live in rural Greene County with my wife, Rhonda, and children, Matthew, Laura, and Bonnie.

KITT PEAK

AL SARRANTONIO

Retirement does not agree with former lieutenant Thomas Mullin. So when he receives a whiskey-stained letter detailing the disappearance of his friend's daughter Abby, he jumps on the first train to Arizona. Folks around town think Abby has gone back to the reservation where she was raised, yet the more Mullin investigates, the more suspicious he becomes. But even his agile mind and gift for deduction can't prepare him for the wild legends of the Papagos or the terrifying truth of what's really in store for Abby.

Dorchester Publishing Co., Inc.
P.O. Box 6640 ___5641-0
Wayne, PA 19087-8640 $5.99 US/$7.99 CAN

Please add $2.50 for shipping and handling for the first book and $.75 for each additional book. NY and PA residents, add appropriate sales tax. No cash, stamps, or CODs. Canadian orders require an extra $2.00 for shipping and handling and must be paid in U.S. dollars. Prices and availability subject to change. **Payment must accompany all orders.**

Name: _____

Address: _____

City: _____ State: _____ Zip: _____

E-mail: _____

I have enclosed $_____ in payment for the checked book(s).

CHECK OUT OUR WEBSITE! www.dorchesterpub.com
_____ Please send me a free catalog.

#50
WILDERNESS

PEOPLE OF THE FOREST

SPECIAL GIANT EDITION!
David Thompson

When Nate King chose a new valley in which to build his home, he wanted to get away from all civilization and the inevitable trouble it brings. But Nate can't duck trouble for very long. A hostile band of Indians has also laid claim to the Kings' valley, and they've made it clear they're not willing to share. In a desperate act to punish Nate and his family, they capture his daughter, Evelyn. And Nate will do anything it takes—even if it means sacrificing his own life—to get her back.

Dorchester Publishing Co., Inc.
P.O. Box 6640
_____5712-3
Wayne, PA 19087-8640
$6.99 US/$8.99 CAN

Please add $2.50 for shipping and handling for the first book and $.75 for each additional book. NY and PA residents, add appropriate sales tax. No cash, stamps, or CODs. Canadian orders require an extra $2.00 for shipping and handling and must be paid in U.S. dollars. Prices and availability subject to change. **Payment must accompany all orders.**

Name: _____

Address: _____

City: _____ State: _____ Zip: _____

E-mail: _____

I have enclosed $_____ in payment for the checked book(s).

CHECK OUT OUR WEBSITE! www.dorchesterpub.com.
_____ Please send me a free catalog.

MAX BRAND®

MOUNTAIN STORMS

Tommy Parks was only twelve when his father's death left him completely alone in the harsh wilderness. And now rumors have begun to trickle down the mountainside: that there's a wild man who can move as silently as the shadows. Yet even Tommy can't live in complete isolation. Every now and then the settlers find a store of bacon or boxes of ammo replaced with pelts. But some aren't satisfied with the generous payment. Some want to hunt Tommy down like an animal. Tommy may have learned the laws of nature, but he's about to find out that his fellow man can be much more dangerous.

BLOOD BROTHERS

COTTON SMITH

Former Texas Ranger John Checker is ready to go home to Dodge City. He and his friends have survived—barely—a bloody battle with Checker's half-brother, Star McCallister, and his gang. But heading home and getting there alive are two different things. They have some mighty dangerous territory to cross first, and McCallister has his own plans for Checker…plans that involve two hired killers.

SHANNON: U.S. MARSHAL
Charles E. Friend

Clay Shannon has decided he's done carrying a star. All he wants is the peace and quiet of a small ranch he can call his own. But then the government names him a U.S. Marshal. Suddenly he finds himself mixed up with a mysterious gambler who has the look of a gunfighter and a man named "King" Kruger, who's determined to grab land any way he can. From back-shooters to bushwhackers, cattle rustling to murder, Shannon may find he's resting in peace much sooner than he planned.

Dorchester Publishing Co., Inc.
P.O. Box 6640
Wayne, PA 19087-8640

_____5682-8
$5.99 US/$7.99 CAN

RIDERS OF THE PURPLE SAGE
ZANE GREY

Zane Grey's masterpiece, *Riders of the Purple Sage*, is one of the greatest, most influential novels of the West ever written. But for nearly a century it has existed only in a profoundly censored version, one that undermined the truth of the characters and distorted Grey's intentions.

Finally the story has been restored from Grey's original handwritten manuscript and the missing and censored material has been reinserted. At long last the classic saga of the gunman known only as Lassiter and his search for his lost sister can be read exactly as Zane Grey wrote it. After all these years, here is the **real** *Riders of the Purple Sage*!
